# Kevan Bevan
## and the BMX
# TIME-LOOP

*Hope you enjoy it!*

*M. Eccles*

# Matthew Eccles

For my beautiful children

xxx

# Chapter 1

Kevan Bevan ducked a flying metal chair and decided: this was the best day of his life.

It was better than the Christmas he got *Super Mario Bros* and played it until his thumb blistered. Or the lunchtime that Mr Carter slipped on a chip and landed on his backside. It was better, even, than when his best mate Anish Desai snorted milk out of his nose. Actually, those last two examples were moments apart, but the point was, no amount of white snot exploding from anyone's nostrils could beat ringside seats for "Bev 'n' Dez" at Wrestlemania Six.

They were only feet away when Mr Perfect performed a pile-driver on Brutus "The Barber" Beefcake. They could also hear, over the noise of tens of thousands of fans, excited commentary from Gorilla Monsoon and Jesse "The Body" Ventura. Even getting sprayed with sweat and baby oil – when "Hacksaw" Jim Duggan punched Dino Bravo in the face – couldn't ruin their fun.

But an Earthquake could.

Hacksaw was Kevan's favourite wrestler, and after an eternity of elbow drops, clotheslines and gurnings, he was finally going to pin Bravo. He started playing to the crowd, standing on the middle rope of each turnbuckle, flicking his mullet, readying his famous call.

But then the floor began to shake.

The "Earthquake" in question was actually eight feet and 10 tonnes of bearded barbarian in a leotard, rumbling into

1

the ring and pushing the referee over the top rope. He sucker-punched Hacksaw and kept him on the canvas under his boot, until Bravo recovered and climbed onto a turnbuckle, ready to jump.

Time seemed to slow; the roar of the crowd became a washing echo, and the camera flashbulbs winked lazily, like in the movies. Kevan pushed past Anish and vaulted the safety barrier. Bravo leapt – Kevan slid under the bottom rope and bounced to his feet, with Bravo hovering above, his arms and legs spread wide, his chest puffed out. Kevan caught Bravo in mid-air and flung him at Earthquake, who pinned Bravo with his bulk. Time gathered pace; the cheers of the crowd grew shrill once more, and the referee slid back in and counted Bravo out.

Hacksaw groggily got to his feet, realised what had happened, and grabbed Kevan's arm. He lifted it into the air, parading Kevan around the ring to blinding camera flashes and a crowd united in hysteria. Hacksaw waved an American flag and finally yelled his famous call, which the crowd echoed:

'Hoh-oh!'

Kevan gave Anish a "Hacksaw" thumbs-up, and his best mate returned the gesture, eyes and mouth wide open. Gorilla Monsoon and Jesse "The Body" Ventura rose behind their commentary desk and yelled into their mics:

'Who is this young hero who has saved Hacksaw from the dreaded Earthquake?'

'I've got the seating plan, Gorilla – he's eleven years old and he hails... from Wales.'

'Hails from Wales? What's his name?'

'Kevan.' Ventura said this less gruff, a bit more melodic.

'Just Kevan?'

'Kevan Bevan!'

'Ventura, that's a convincing Welsh accent you've got there–'

'Wakey, wakey, Kevan Bevan!'

Kevan opened his eyes and looked up. Above him stood Mr Carter, looking only slightly less amused than Kevan's classmates.

'Good afternoon, young man. Feel rested?'

He'd done it again – his daydream had turned into an actual dream.

Kevan lifted his head from his desk, a page from his wrestling magazine clinging to his cheek. The teacher peeled the page off and started flipping through it. He glanced at Kevan as he held the magazine out sideways; a section unfolded and hung down.

'That's not the kind of flesh I was braced for, Master Bevan,' Mr Carter said, before the class giggled at the A3 poster of the Ultimate Warrior, flexing greasily amid his luminous tassels. Kevan's cheeks burned and a film of sweat grew onto his forehead and palms. He shot Anish a look – he was supposed to nudge him if Mr Carter came near – so his so-called best mate hastily leant away from Kevan's steady gaze, revealing Ieuan "Ya-Ya" Roberts at the desk across the aisle, wiggling his eyebrows under his perfectly-quiffed centre-parting.

'Off at the wrestling were you, Master Bevan? Well, just to make sure you've fully returned, could you tell us all where you are now?'

Kevan glared at his desk and noted – as if for the first time – the dirty brown grain of the heavy wooden lid, the pen groove running along the back hinge, the old-fashioned inkpot hole which he hoped to fill with bubble-gum by the end of the summer term.

'I'll help you out, shall I? We are in Seven Carter, Valley Hill Primary School. And we don't practice suplexes and clotheshorses; we expand our knowledge. We fire up our imaginations. We strive–'

The home-time bell rang – the class leapt as one.

'We strive to put our chairs on our desks before we leave.'

Chairs rose and banged onto lids before the class streamed toward the door by the cloakroom corridor. Mr Carter opened it and tapped each on the head, chanting 'homework'.

Kevan and Anish's desks were near the window so they were the last two out. Anish got the tap; Kevan's head, however, was gripped firmly.

'Master Bevan, a word?'

Mr Carter turned Kevan round by his head and directed him back into the room. Anish backed out and, once Mr Carter had closed the door, peered through the glass, his big anxious eyes shining in the dark corridor.

'Have you made a start on your homework yet, Master Bevan?'

Kevan squinted and opened his mouth slightly.

Mr Carter lifted a long white stick from behind his desk, held one end, and rested the other end in his left palm.

'Do you remember what it was?'

That question was below the belt – he'd set it a whole week ago. Kevan inspected his battered shoes.

'That's a no then,' Mr Carter said, nodding at the floor. He approached, tapping the stick into his left palm. Kevan stepped back; Mr Carter turned toward the high windows and used the stick to close them.

'Let's go back in time – shall we? – to last week. I told you all that a museum is going to be opened on the site of the old mine. Your class project was to write about the mine.'

He turned to lean his stick against the blackboard, so Kevan took the opportunity to flick Vs at Anish.

Mr Carter perched on the edge of his desk.

'Now, I know about your family and its… history.'

'You mean when the mine blew up,' Kevan mumbled. He hated when people talked around it.

Mr Carter nodded, but his head wobbled from side to side – not so much a 'Yes' as a 'Kind of'.

'And that is why I asked you to write instead about the coal itself, and why it's – why it was – the envy of the world.'

Kevan nodded back. He understood now why he'd forgotten.

It was boring.

'Kevan, if you were able to get your head out of the clouds from time to time, and apply yourself, you could be in many of the same classes as Master Desai when you go to Valley Hill Secondary in September. Don't you want that?'

This was a trap that all grown-ups set. Of course he wanted to be in the same classes as Anish; but if Kevan said 'yes' to this, Mr Carter would decide that it meant 'yes' to lots of other things – like doing schoolwork. Concentrating. Behaving. You name it.

So he shrugged.

Mr Carter smiled and folded his arms.

'Perhaps September's too far away. So, let's come back to the immediate future. Your homework is due tomorrow – Friday, the 30th day of March, in The Year Of Our Heavenly Headmaster Nineteen Hundred and Ninety – and I would strongly advise you to do it.'

Mr Carter nodded at the door: lecture over. But Kevan didn't move; he instead grimaced at his magazine on the teacher's desk. Mr Carter rolled it up and bopped Kevan on the head.

'And no more magazines.' He handed it over.

Kevan turned on his heel to face his desk, then the door, then back to his desk. He grimaced again; Mr Carter sighed and nodded. Kevan scurried over, took his chair off, opened the desk lid and, with great care, lifted out around fifteen wrestling and computer game magazines.

But the magazines slipped from his arms and he flailed, knocking Anish's chair off the side of the desk, which in turn banged against Ya-Ya's chair, and soon there was a domino rally of chairs, all bouncing into and off one another, before clattering to the floor.

Mr Carter surveyed the aisles, cluttered with skyward-pointing metal legs. After an age he spoke.

'See you tomorrow, Master Bevan,' he said brightly.

Out the door, coat off the hook, across the hall, past the infant's library, the echo of Kevan's steps on the parquet floor chasing him, until he was clear of the main entrance and out in the open. He posed at the top step, hands on hips, legs apart, 'scanning the crowd' – two departing infants with parents, and his best mate Anish, waiting patiently – then ran down the steps, giving high-fives to the saplings that split the playground in two.

Anish's navy Parka was even darker against the primary colours of the new climbing frame, but his black hair shone like an over-washed beacon in the spring sun. He began wrapping his chain below the saddle of his new mountain bike, a smart, red, 12-gear Emmelle Leopard. Kevan's BMX had seen better days – the yellow rubber handlebars now had murky green creeping in, and the ends were broken away to reveal the rust-spotted metal underneath. On the other hand, Anish's bike was rubbish at kerb endos, as Kevan had discovered on his first (and probably last) go on it.

'What did Mr Carter say?'

'Blah blah homework blah,' Kevan said, grabbing his bike from the railings.

'And what did you say?' Anish asked, the serious tone betrayed by the hint of mischief in his eyes.

Kevan peered at Anish.

'I said...'

Kevan threw his bike to the ground, pulled his elasticated tie up around his head at the temple, clenched his fists and tensed his arms, so that they curved taut.

'I said–' he repeated in a bad American accent, shaking a finger at Anish, '–"Mister Carter, you are a farter! And I don't just mean a little ol' squeak! I mean a raspin', blastin', everlastin' bottom burp! The kind that knocks grannies over! The kind that shatters windows! The kind that stops time!

'"A-and when I'm through with you at Wrestlemania Six at the... thingumajig arena, you'll be as flat as a pancake! As dead as a dodo! And there will be no nee-eed for this stupid, pointless, waste-of-time homework!"'

Kevan leapt onto the railings and thrashed against them, puffing out his cheeks and roaring. He only stopped when he saw he'd been thrusting his pelvis at a pavement-bound pensioner.

Anish gave him an eye-roll/head-shake one-two. Kevan decided to get him involved.

'"Desai-co" is running scared! "The Bev-astator" smells blood!'

'No, no, Bev – come on–'

Kevan leapt down and grabbed Anish's hand, clamping it against his own neck. Time to test the new rubber tarmac.

Kevan kicked his own legs forward into the air and landed hard on his back. He closed his eyes but kept up the commentary:

'Bevastator's on the mat! What's Desaico gonna do?'

Kevan opened an eye and craned his neck. Anish stood over him, still shaking his head slowly.

'What's – Desaico – gonna–'

Anish sighed, flung up an arm and elbow-dropped Kevan. '–doo-hooh-oo-ooh!'

Anish lay across Kevan and slapped the ground, getting into it.

'One!'

'Can the Bevastator break free?'

'Two!'

'Is Desaico too strong?'

'Three!'

Another heavy blow to Kevan's chest, but not from Anish. Someone else now lay on them, an elbow waggling near Kevan's head, and he knew, from the smell of biscuits, that it was Hughesy.

'Pile-on!'

And then Ieuan "Ya-Ya" Roberts's face appeared above Kevan, blotting out the sun, his centre-parted fringe bouncing over his bright eyes as he landed atop Hughesy.

Anish gasped; Kevan began to wriggle furiously.

'Gerroff!'

The core of the pile-on failed, and Kevan scrambled to his feet. Ya-Ya took his time getting up, laughing hard. He flicked his head back and his perfect fringe settled into a symmetrical chicane.

'It wasn't a pile-on, Ya-Ya,' Kevan protested, ignoring the fact that a pile-on exists the moment someone shouts it.

'Bonking then, was it?'

'We were wrestling.'

'Who are you meant to be?' Ya-Ya scoffed, glancing at Kevan's bulk. 'Big Daddy?'

'We were doing Main Event.'

'That wasn't Main Event,' he sneered, 'and I should know cos I get it on satellite.'

Kevan let the boast slide, but Ya-Ya tried again.

'I'll probably watch Wrestlemania live.'

'Yeah?' Kevan said, leaving the "so" silent.

'Isn't it on at two in the morning?' Anish wondered.

'Yeah, but I can stay up as late as I want,' Ya-Ya said, as if everyone in Valley Hill knew this.

'Can I come?' Hughesy asked, his curly brown hair bouncing in the breeze.

'No chance,' snorted Ya-Ya.

Kevan stood next to Anish, arms folded, a united front. 'We're taping it to watch later.'

'Are we?' Anish asked.

'Yeah, course,' Kevan said, gazing resolutely at Ya-Ya.

Anish nodded, then frowned. 'How?'

'My Dad's workmate,' Kevan hissed.

'You lovebirds,' Ya-Ya said, grinning again. 'So, you're borrowing a video. Now you just need to borrow a video player.'

He brushed past Kevan and nudged Anish's bike so that it scraped down and rattled onto the ground. Anish crouched by his beloved Emmelle. He looked up at Kevan and shook his head.

'It's scratched.'

There was only one thing Kevan could do.

He snorted back a big ball of spit and hocked it forward onto the middle of his tongue, before blowing it out – *wupthuhhhh*. It looped high over the railings and landed

9

twenty feet from Ya-Ya's heels. Anish spat too, but hesitantly, and a thin white string whipped out of his mouth and swung down onto his shirt front from his chin.

His big eyes darted to Kevan's, the spit string bowing like a Tarzan vine, and they started to laugh. Kevan stopped when he saw Mr Carter through the classroom window, holding a chair and frowning.

# Chapter 2

"JESUS SAVES

*...BUT RUSH SCORES ON THE REBOUND!'*

Kevan and Anish used this graffitied sign outside the Methodist Church as their road-crossing point every day. Anish thought it was hilarious even though he didn't like football.

They crossed, and pedalled along the gap between the community hall and the Conservative Club, through the small arch in the town wall, past the fishmonger and sweetshop in the pebbled alley, until they were out onto Bumptown high street.

Kevan hopped his bike into the road and got a beep from a purple Montego; Anish stuck his arm out and cycled slowly on the pavement. Then past the Kwik Save, past the curtain shop, past the Freeman Hardy Willis (which Kevan had renamed to an unrepeatable version), until they reached the Amusements.

Kevan slowed. Ya-Ya would often be in there, but Kevan wasn't looking for him; he was looking for Ya-Ya's older sister.

A group of teenagers was gathered by a slot machine. Somebody moved away to get more change.

And there she was.

Amid the rows of gamblers and games machines, her dark hair backlit by the flashing amber of an Each-Way Nudger, was Gwen Roberts: her school tie, like her skirt, short and thin, her bright white trainers defiant amid the cigarette haze.

She was fourteen and went to the secondary on the other side of town, between the miner's terraces and the roads near Kevan's house, so Kevan had few chances to get her attention. Most Saturday afternoons Gwen could be found at the Amusements, or in the new shopping arcade across the road. Kevan was limited in what he could do to impress her but he always tried his best: pulling a wheely down the high street, getting chased by PC Richards (on one occasion, both), but she never noticed.

'You know I don't like the name "Desaico",' Anish said, now caught up.

'I know,' Kevan said, his gaze unwavering, 'but the other one–'

'"The Anish-thetist",' Anish said, proudly.

'Yeah. That one,' Kevan murmured. 'It's a bit of a mouthful.'

'Yeah, but my special move–'

'–is the sleeper hold. Yeah yeah, I get it.' Gwen moved out of sight, so Kevan turned to his best mate. 'It's not catchy enough. Hardly anyone knows what an Anaeste – eashther... what one of them is.'

'It's *my* name, Bev.'

'Sorry, dude,' Kevan shrugged. 'Desaico is just... easier to say.'

Kevan pedalled on, the bunting from last year's Harvest Festival criss-crossing overhead. The high street sloped down toward the main town gateway, and with the wind at his

12

back Kevan shot through the pedestrian arch. He turned right at the lights and freewheeled downhill, at times holding his arms out, savouring that sweet space between school and home, where no-one could nag him. The buffering air cleared the voices, and he looked out, past the descending rooftops and the green-barked promise of the budding trees, to the western valley slopes, wondering briefly what lay beyond them.

He waited for Anish by the bungalows and they wheeled across the playing fields, coming out by the adventure playground, and through all of this Anish hassled Kevan about the wrestling tape, and what night he could come round, and to make sure he asked his dad as soon as possible, and to make sure he did his homework. So much for that sweet space.

Anish disappeared into his big bay-windowed house, and Kevan cycled on, arms folded, weaving only slightly, out of Anish's street, down the Old West Road and onto Meifod Crescent. Kevan's house lay just before the turning circle of the cul-de-sac; a small, pinky-beige end-terrace with a crack running diagonally down from the side of the house to the top of the porch.

Kevan wheeled his bike alongside the dull-blue Sierra on the driveway and flung it into the front garden, catching a couple of nodding daffodils, and one closed tulip. He opened the outer porch door and closed it heavily, but Fenwick didn't come. The dog was getting pretty deaf.

'Wipe your feet,' came Mam's flat, ordered voice from inside. Kevan did a quick shuffle on the "Wellcome" mat and flung the inner door open. The cushioned crash against coats was answered by the lackadaisical chink of Fenwick's collar, followed by a brief glint of his gold coat as he *click-clack*ed off the kitchen lino and padded onto the hallway carpet.

13

Kevan dropped and rolled into Fenwick. 'Get off me! Get off me!' he protested, trying to prompt some kind of slobbery assault. The Labrador probed him once with his nose and panted.

The draught from the open door drew a gust of burning charcoal from the garden, along with the start of "Back to Life" by Soul II Soul from the radio. Dad popped his head through the back door, his moustache wiggling as he blew on his fingers.

'Barbie time!' he yelled through to Kevan, waggling his hand. He had a habit of squirting lighter fluid onto the lit coals for no reason.

'On tonight's menu – flame-grilled Dad,' Kevan said.

Mam's head appeared from the pantry in front of Dad's, the straight fringe of her new bob hairdo hiding her raised eyebrows, as she inspected Kevan's appearance. 'Well, you won't be eating flame-grilled anything until you've washed your hands,' she said, before disappearing.

Kevan hopped up the stairs to his bedroom. The metal handles of his rickety MFI wardrobe rattled with each step, and reached a crescendo when he dropped his rucksack and coat against the drawers.

He remembered taking home some kind of textbook last week. It was here somewhere... there, midway down his pile of comics, between a Dandy and a Buster. He reached out for the thin hardback and placed it next to his blue exercise book, but the reflection of Wendy James in his wardrobe mirror made him turn.

The smaller posters on his wall were either wrestling or *Smash Hits* magazine pullouts, but there were two big A1 posters. The one above his bed was Batman, and the one on his door was Transvision Vamp.

Or rather, Wendy James.

She was mega-cool, all peroxide hair, bright pink lipstick, black top with straps, leant against a wall, expressionless behind classic black sunglasses. Gwen was cool like that too, like nothing bothered her. Maybe she liked "The Vamp".

'What's that, Wend? Just ten minutes on Metroid?'

In an instant, with white noise on his little telly, Kevan sat on his bed with his game controller in hand. He listened out for Mam and Dad – Mam was talking about tomorrow's tea, and Dad was calling it a 'feast', but in a sarcastic way. Probably Chicken Surprise.

He glanced at Batman, cloaked apart from his piercing glare.

'Don't look at me, Michael Keaton – Wendy said it was fine.'

Kevan opened up a scrap of paper which had the 24-digit code he'd have to put in to start where he'd left off on his game – fighting some dinosaur-alien thing.

Then Mam's voice leapt up the stairs:

'I said go wash your hands! I won't ask you again.'

How could she even hear what he was doing? He stayed still for a moment, before pressing the "Power" button, but steps began at the foot of the stairs. Kevan stood and flung his controller onto the duvet.

'Okay, okay! I'm going.' He stomped to the bathroom to head off another nag.

One day it would be nice if, when Mam said she wouldn't ask again, she meant it.

★

'You should've seen it, pal,' Dad said, waving his barbecue tongs in the cool spring air like he was conducting an orchestra. 'There were like twenty aisles.'

15

The wind had changed; the barbecue smoke swirled over the fence into number 13's back garden, and Kevan got a brief respite in the heady fragrance of the number 17's freshly-cut grass, the first of the year.

'Dad.'

'They had a pharmacy. They had a café.' And then, poking his tongs with each word: 'They even sold socks.'

'Dad.'

'Socks, Kev. In a supermarket.'

'Mam is going to kill you.'

Dad shook his head and raised an eyebrow. He produced a wrapper – "Marsden's Own 8 Thick Pork Sausages" – and nodded to the barbecue a few feet away.

'I'm gonna cook your mam these bangers and burgers, and when she says how good they taste, I'll tell her where I got 'em, and then she'll be sold.'

'Who'll be sold?' Mam asked, putting a magazine and a mug of tea down on the dirty-white garden table.

'You,' Dad said, 'Or part exchange for a newer model.' He winked at Kevan.

Mam zipped up her coat and inspected his shorts and T-shirt.

'Is that why you dressed like you're auditioning for Wham?'

'Just enjoying the sunshine, my love.'

'The clocks went forward a week ago and you're already in Club Tropicana,' she said before sitting down.

'And I'm making the most of it. 'Cos it's "Club Chicken Surprise" tomorrow.'

'It gets funnier every time,' Mam said, as she gazed at her magazine. Kevan's pride at correctly guessing tomorrow's tea was tempered by the fact that he'd have to eat it.

Mam turned a page. 'You know what else is funny? I can't remember the last time I heard mention of homework in this house.'

Busted.

'You talking to me?' Kevan enquired.

She looked up from her magazine, mirth making pretty creases around her eyes. 'No, darling, your dad.'

'Done mine, Mam,' Dad said, raising his beer to his lips.

'Seems like ages since you had any.'

'Seems like longer since he did any.'

Kevan's mind scrambled: say you've done it, then you'll have to do it later, and no *Metroid*. Say there isn't any and you won't be able to do any later. And if you didn't do it, and they found out–

Fenwick barked and leapt heavily onto the patio before plodding into the kitchen. Kevan saw an "out", and began to follow the dog in.

'Fen – where are you going?'

But Mam was a pro.

'Kevan Bevan–'

Time to play his trump card.

'I'm sure Fen's going deaf.'

'He's not the only one.'

'Hey, Dad, was there a vets in Marsdens when you went?'

Dad stood, mouth agape as Mam's head slowly turned toward him. Kevan darted into the kitchen to avoid the carnage.

He blinked in the sudden gloom – the dog was sat at the inner porch door, his tail wagging. His eyes twinkled as he glanced back.

'What is it boy?'

Fen frowned at Kevan, then resumed his vigil at the door, panting at the grotty net curtain that covered it. Kevan's head throbbed; he shouldn't have leapt onto the patio so quickly.

'For god's sake, Andrew – I told you I don't want to go to that big supermarket.' She'd used his full name.

Kevan came back out. Mam was holding the sausage wrapper.

'I know, I know,' Dad said, his beer and tongs raised almost like an offering. 'But it's on the way. And you should have seen it Ruthie – they even had a travel agents.'

'We don't need a travel agents to go to Barmouth.'

Dad glanced at Kevan. His argument had fallen flat and he scrambled for another.

'Socks,' he spluttered, desperate. Mam squinted at him briefly.

'We get everything we need from the high street,' she said.

'This meat is half the price of Roberts's,' Dad said.

'That's because it's half the meat,' Mam shot back, and looked down at the magazine to end the conversation.

Dad handed a sausage in a bun to Kevan. 'Judas,' he muttered.

Dad's mention of Roberts's made Kevan realise he needed to side with Dad; if they shopped at Marsdens, they would stop going to the butchers on Saturdays. Ya-Ya's dad owned the butchers. Ya-Ya was in there sometimes, when Kevan had gone with Dad. No more butchers = much less Ya-Ya.

Kevan took a bite: the skin cracked and the meat gave too easily. And it smelt... off.

'Mmm,' he said.

Kevan sat at the end of his bed with the textbook on his lap. He ran his hand over the plastic coating, bubbled in places. If he just got the homework done now, that would stop the nagging.

He had his blue exercise book open already – he just needed a pen. He went into Mam's bedroom and grabbed the one on her bedside table, next to the notepad and telephone. He looked up and slowly approached the window.

A building company called "Pro Construction" had bought the fields from the end of their cul-de-sac all the way down to the creek at the bottom. They'd built a few houses down there, but up this end all they'd done is knock down the cottage at the head of the turning circle, for a road that hadn't been laid. At some point they would cut down the stand of trees at the far edge of the field, but for now they remained. Which was good news for Mam – she reckoned that with them gone, she would be able to see, from her bedroom window, the distant headstock and wheel above the old mineshaft.

Mr Carter couldn't not mention Granddad – what happened was a big thing in the town. And Kevan didn't mind writing about it, but Mr Carter had steered him away from the subject. So now he was writing about coal.

He came back to his room, flicked to the next blank page of his lined workbook and wrote on the top left-hand corner: "Thursday 29th March 1990". One line below: "School Project"; and the next: "Valley Hill Coal".

He looked up; reflected in his little mirror was Wendy James, her eyebrows rising just above her sunglasses. She appeared to be shrugging.

# Chapter 3

Dad clumped past, bending quickly, opening kitchen cupboards. Kevan yawned over his mushy cornflakes, a proper jaw-clicker like Fenwick did sometimes. He hadn't slept well. At one point he'd woken, moaning into his pillow. He had a hazy memory – or was it a dream? – of Dad on the landing, half-lit by the bathroom light, his voice a murmur – 'You alright pal?' – and he'd answered, his own voice sounding like it wasn't part of his body.

There were two possible reasons he'd slept badly – either because the sausages disagreed with him, or because he hadn't done his homework. Probably both.

'Have you been nicking biscuits?' Mam said, her voice buzzing around behind Kevan.

'No,' he mumbled.

'Well, no Kit Kat for you, in any case.' She turned to Dad, bopping a slipper at his builder's bum. 'And what are you looking for?'

'...my clipboard...'

'It'll be in your bag,' she said, taking her cup to the sink. 'And leave the biscuits alone – they're for Kevan at break-time.'

'What? I haven't touched the biscuits. And my clipboard isn't in my bag. I'm not stupid.'

'This is what happens when you drink. Disorganised.'

Dad stood up straight and held out two fingers. 'I had two beers.' His fingers turned into Vs.

'And ratty.' Mam winked at Kevan. Dad grabbed her shoulders and she jumped around like a ragdoll; the usual Monty Python routine, all for Kevan's amusement. He smiled but it felt like a flat line across his face.

'You okay?' Mam asked.

Kevan desperately wanted to tell them. It might even be better for them to know now, so that he wouldn't have to tell them when he got back from school.

'I know what'll cheer him up,' Dad said, his arm around Mam's shoulders, his hairy mitt dangling over her collarbone. 'I'll get Shane to tape that wrestling thing for you. You've been banging on about it long enough.'

'Well, I'm not sure he's earned it,' Mam said.

Kevan tensed his jaw.

'Why?' Dad said, frowning.

Here we go.

'Because your son left muddy footprints everywhere yesterday.'

'Ah, my son, is it?' Dad exclaimed.

Kevan had dodged it again. He rose from the table and went to his bedroom for his rucksack. Well, he wouldn't dodge it at school.

Or with Anish, for that matter. It was raining, which meant Anish wasn't allowed to use his bike, which meant they both walked to school, which meant no escape from the Dezzy Third Degree. Whatever "Third Degree" meant.

'Dad said I can come over on a weeknight next week.' Anish would always start from a different topic before zig-zagging to the real subject, but Kevan wasn't going to make it easy for him.

'Okay.'

'So, when are you getting the tape?'

'Dunno. Probably Tuesday.'

'Okay. Can you check?'

'Yes, Dezzy.'

'Okay.'

'Okay.'

They walked on in silence for a while, the rain crackling on Anish's cagoule. Any moment now, he was going to ask about the homework, and then there would be a barrage of questions, and guilt, and sulks. Any moment now.

Crackle crackle.

'What did you have for tea?'

'I didn't do the homework, Anish. Alright? I played Metroid instead, and now I'm gonna get done. Happy now?'

They walked on in the drizzle, Anish one step behind. He muttered a 'No,' and then, 'Why would I be happy? We won't be in the same classes at Secondary.'

They stopped across the road from the adventure playground and fields. Kevan glanced at Anish's poor, miserable mug.

'Dezzy, I'm just not as clever as you. Even if they put us in the same sets, I'd just get moved down.'

Anish nodded, his mouth curled over at one side.

'Look, we're gonna be best mates forever. Alright? Just like we said.'

Anish nodded again, and stepped off the kerb, but Kevan braced him with his forearm and pointed across the road.

Ya-Ya was at the adventure playground, calling up at whoever was in the pirate's cabin. A scared little kid, probably. Hughesy was rocking on the springy horse thing, his curly hair bouncing around.

Anish's body stiffened against Kevan's hand; this happened whenever he saw Ya-Ya.

Kevan didn't used to pay Ya-Ya any mind. He was mean, and sarcastic, and seemed to treat his "friends" with as much respect as his enemies, but aside from the odd name, such as "pauper" or "podge", he mainly left Kevan alone. And then, two-and-a-half years ago, came Anish's first day at Valley Hill Primary.

They all played out for lunch that day, and a group naturally formed around Anish. This happened with every new pupil. The time it took the novelty to wear off was proportionate to the distance from Valley Hill from which they'd initially come. Roughly it was: from somewhere in the Valley = a day or two. From somewhere else in Wales = perhaps a week. England = that differed depending on who you were; it ranged from a day to a fortnight. But according to Miss Daniels Anish was originally from India, despite Anish insisting he was from Bradford. Either way, the novelty of this kind of newcomer was untested in Kevan's class.

The interrogation continued.

'Is your Dad from India?'

'Yes.'

'Is your Mam?'

Anish had a look of bemusement on his face.

'No. She's from Bradford.'

Ya-Ya's face contorted into theatrical confusion.

'She's white.'

Ya-Ya became more animated, like this revelation gave him more fuel.

'So you're half-and-half then.'

And this was when Anish began to stiffen. He was like a statue.

'What's that?' Rachel said.

'He's half-caste,' Hughesy said, matter-of-factly.

'What's *that?*' Rachel asked again.

Ya-Ya sneered. 'My Dad calls it half-and-half. So... if your mam's English and your dad's an Indian, then you're–' and a lightbulb went off in Ya-Ya's hateful little brain – 'You're like chips *and* rice.'

The group started laughing. At the time Kevan thought it was pretty funny, for Ya-Ya. But then he saw the look on Anish's face and his own cheeks burned. It was the same face Little Owen pulled when he wet himself in Year 1. Like he wanted to be teleported anywhere else in the world. Anish later explained to Kevan that it wasn't the insult that made him stiffen; it was the fact that Ya-Ya already knew his Mam was white, because they'd entered his dad's butcher's the Saturday before and Ya-Ya was there, staring across the counter at them. He'd deliberately drawn it out in front of everyone so he could pick on him.

Kevan's family was mixed but in a different way. His Welsh Granddad – Kevan – was actually Irish. *His* Mam and Dad moved to England, shortly before the war. And Kevan's Bristol Grandparents were actually Welsh, but his own Dad was actually English even though he lived in Wales. It was all very confusing. And, like Anish, he only had his Mam and Dad in Valley Hill. No other family. No other generations. No roots.

'If he's chips and rice, then what am I?' Kevan heard himself say.

'What? You're nothing, Bevan.'

'No – my mam's Welsh and my dad's English. My first name's Irish. So what am I? Flippin' – chips and – and – and – Jacket Potato?!'

It made no sense, but Kevan had said jacket potato really posh, and the group was in hysterics. People started repeating his phrasing of jacket potato. Ya-Ya's cruelty had been broken down.

It was Anish's first day in school, and it was Kevan's first day standing up to Ya-Ya. It seemed easy at the time. He didn't realise that this was the only time it would feel that way.

Despite this, ever since, Kevan had sought to protect Anish in whatever way he could: yelling the correct pronunciation of his name whenever people said it wrong; stepping up to Ya-Ya whenever he tried to physically intimidate Anish; in fact, trying to fix things for him any time he could. Most of the time, Anish let him. And even though they were probably going to be in different classes at Secondary, nothing would change that.

Soon Ya-Ya and Hughesy moved away from the pirate's cabin, across the playing fields. Anish's body relaxed; Kevan released Anish and they began to cross the road.

'That was like a backward clothesline,' Kevan remarked, trying to change the subject. But as soon as he said it, something – from the far reaches of the very back of his mind – nagged at him. He'd felt it at breakfast too, but he wasn't quite sure what it was.

'Do you think Mr Carter will give you an Action Slip?'

Kevan huffed. Anish was such a misery-guts sometimes. But that creeping feeling popped up again as they reached the kerb. There seemed to be something, some connection, he was missing.

'He thinks he's so cool with satellite,' Kevan said, nodding over at a distant Ya-Ya. 'He doesn't even like wrestling.'

'Bev.'

'He'll only watch it so he can show off.'

'Bev, if you get another Action Slip–'

'Hughesy only plays with him, because – because...'

'–won't you get grounded?'

Kevan stopped on the pavement, his brow knotting. 'Yeah – that's what happened before.'

Kevan's knees twitched as Anish continued the train of thought.

'–and if you get grounded–'

Kevan clapped his hand over Anish's mouth to stop any more words coming out, but he said it himself anyway.

'Wrestlemania – No!'

Right then, staring into Anish Desai's fearful eyes, Kevan Bevan's life hit rock bottom.

Then a car raced past and sprayed a huge, gritty puddle onto them.

Okay, *now* it was rock bottom.

# Chapter 4

Assembly was damp, the windows ghostly with condensation. Mr Carter was on the piano playing "If I Had A Hammer". There were sixty cross-legged children either end of the hall and Mrs Peters, the Headmistress, stalked the parquet in the middle.

Years four to seven were at the far end – the "gym" end, near the wooden bars and stacked benches – and Kevan usually held his *Come & Praise* songbook in front of his mouth and mortified Anish with his own renditions of the songs, which ranged from the absurd ("If I Had A Hammock"), to the offensive ("If I Had A _____"), or he would emphasise the wrong words, or rise in pitch to the end of each line. He had an array of skills. But today, he sang in tune, and in time.

He'd had three Action Slips in his life, all from Mr Carter. One was for swearing, one was for shoving someone, and one was for lying, and Mam had grounded him for a week each time. He didn't know whether he'd be given an Action Slip for not doing homework, but with so much at stake, he had to get something in.

Because if he was grounded, it would mean no Wrestlemania for that whole week, and he would find out every result by the time he got to watch it. Little Owen wouldn't be able to contain himself, and Ya-Ya would take great pleasure in ruining it for him, regardless of whether he actually liked wrestling.

Mr Carter didn't take homework out of his tray until they came back in from afternoon break, so Kevan had until then. With two breaks and one lunch, that gave him just over an hour. The homework didn't even have to be any good – he just had to hand something in.

The song ended; Mrs Peters replaced her half-moon glasses and frowned at the book.

'Thank you, Mr Carter, and thank you children, as always, for your beautiful voices. Although I do still find the last song less like a hymn and more like The Beatles.

'Now, we have a special visitor this morning, and he'd like to talk to you about a special project.'

The infants on the corridor end all twisted round as a suited man with grey hair and glasses took big steps into the hall. Kevan had seen him about, sometimes on the high street, sometimes in the local paper, but he couldn't place him.

'Who's that?' Kevan asked.

'He owns the mine,' Anish whispered.

'The mine?' Kevan peered at him. Big frame, deliberate steps, strange suit. Woolly, but with a kind of glint to it. 'But why–'

'The homework,' Anish hissed.

The man smiled at nearly every single child before he spoke.

'Hello. My name is Mr Protheroe. Like most of you I live in Valley Hill. I was lucky enough to buy the old mine, and I'm turning it into a museum. Now, that might sound a bit strange. But I want you and the children after you to learn from our past.

'Now, I've heard that you have all been working on a project for the museum – drawing pictures, and the like. And some of you have written about the mine, and Mr Carter has

28

invited me to hear you read some of it later. And I may ask your permission to display some of your work in our visitor's centre.'

This homework thing was a big deal. Kevan would have to make an effort.

Once Assembly finished and they filed back to class, he muttered – mainly to himself – that if it was so important, why hadn't anyone reminded him?

And then Anish promptly listed his own efforts:

- Five minutes after Mr Carter set it last Friday;
- Cycling on the high street Saturday (and in the sweetshop);
- Climbing trees down by the creek Sunday (although Kevan forced him to concede that they were both upside-down at the time);
- At break and lunch on Monday;
- After school on Tuesday;
- After school and at Scouts on Wednesday;
- After school yesterday.

Kevan quickly decided they needed to focus instead on solutions.

He formulated a plan: first break they would get started, then lunch would be spent getting the rest written, then second break would be spent making sure it didn't read like it had been scribbled down during first break and lunch. All in all, about an hour or so.

Until Mr Carter spoke.

'We'll be doing our presentation to Mr Protheroe straight after lunch, so make sure you've got it ready.'

Okay – no second break: he had about 50 minutes.

'Master Bevan.'

'Yes Teach-Carter-Sir.' He nearly saluted.

'Have you done your homework?'

The whole class looked at him.

'Yes, sir.'

'Then you will be reading yours first.'

'Thank you, sir,' he said, beaming tightly. No chance to bodge if he didn't finish by lunch. Well, 50 minutes should –

'And indoor break this morning class,' Mr Carter said, to loud groans. He motioned to the rain streaming down the window. 'It's out of my hands. Who will you have to take it up with, Miss Allen?'

'The man in the celestial penthouse, sir?'

'Correct.'

Kevan stared at the rivulets on the window. No breaks. He now had 30-odd minutes, and only then if the rain stopped soon.

★

Kevan checked his Casio watch: 13:20. Anish nervously nibbled on banana bread, half-hidden behind his lunchbox, while Kevan resumed wolfing his Chicken Supreme, glancing at the windows every five seconds for signs of rain. The clouds were getting dark and he was sure he heard the sound of thunder, like distant rockfall.

He ran through backup plans in case the weather did turn bad again. All the plans were inspired by that master of wangles, Winker Watson from his *Dandy* comics: he could confidently reach into his rucksack and pretend he couldn't find it; he could hold up a sheet of A4 and make something up for the reading, and then cobble something together while the rest of the selected pupils did theirs; and then there was a third option, which involved convincing Mr Carter

30

he'd already handed it in and then getting upset that the teacher had 'lost' it. He'd already used this wangle on him back in October '89, so it was a last resort.

First break in the classroom had been all frantic whispers and a botched start; his A4 sheet had his name and the date – backdated, this time – and that was it. Break was over before they even had a chance to get the textbook out. Then Mr Protheroe came in and wittered about the mine for most of what remained of the morning, so Kevan wasn't able to write it then, either. He had to look alert and interested.

Thirty-nine minutes of lunch left; just enough time to fill out a page of A4 with something. They skirted the playground and found a quiet corner at the side of the school building, near the steps to the "Girls" door. Kevan reached into his rucksack for the textbook. He pulled out the magazines he'd taken out of his desk yesterday, gawped at them, then scrabbled into the rucksack, flicking out pens, sweet wrappers, scraps of paper – no textbook.

'Oh no – where is it?' he shouted, mainly at himself, realising he must have mistaken the weight of the mags for the textbook. He grabbed Anish, looked down at his rucksack, then back at him.

'Dezzy, you've got to help me.'

'I *am* helping you.'

Kevan searched his face – Anish knew what he meant.

Anish shook his head. 'I can't, Bev – it's not right!'

'Well, you need to get me a textbook then – they won't let me in during breaks after that thing with the school hamster and the poster paint.'

Anish shook his head rapidly, his tongue lolling.

There was no arguing with that kind of fear. Kevan's jaw set.

'Okay – I'll do it.' Kevan stood.

31

'But Mrs Wells won't let you in.'

Kevan's brow lowered. 'We'll see about that,' he said, and checked his watch: 13:24. He marched with purpose and promptly tripped over his rucksack, before recovering and moving into the main playground.

Both the "Boys" and "Girls" doors were closed at lunch; only the main door was open, and that was at the very front of the building. Each day a dinner lady manned it non-stop, and today it was Mrs Wells.

She was the head dinner lady, she had a ledge for a bosom, and she never drifted more than a few yards from the door. Kevan marched up to her; she shifted her weight to her other leg and peered at him over her big folded arms. He blinked and reset his eyebrows.

'Mr Carter wanted me to help with the presentation.'

A smile appeared at the side of her mouth.

'Okay – I'll take you to him.'

Kevan scrambled for a response, but then a kerfuffle began over at the infants' side. Mrs Wells's eyes darted over. Then Kevan glanced at the source of the noise.

It was a pile-on. Forbidden.

Kevan's eyebrows raised. Mrs Wells's eyes narrowed.

Finally her arms unfolded and she huffed off the steps.

'Hoi,' she barked at the pile of five-year olds.

'Mrs Wells–'

'Go on in, Kevan,' she said, flapping a hand behind her.

Kevan skittered past the infants' library and glanced round the corner into the hall. Mr Carter was at the counter, getting Chicken Supreme. Half of the classrooms opened out to the hall, but Seven Carter had two doors – one into the hall and another into the "Girls" corridor opposite where he now stood. Kevan walked quickly past the tables, into the corridor, past the coats and through that door.

13:28. A quick scan of the classroom – no textbooks. He got to Mr Carter's desk but nothing there, either. Perhaps they were in the stationery cupboard? Kevan glanced through the panes of both doors, and opened Mr Carter's desk drawer. He took out the big key and unlocked the cupboard door.

The cupboard was built into the wall and had a space in the middle, around which was shelving all the way up to the ceiling. He scanned the shelves. Was that the textbooks, up on the left? How anyone could reach the top shelves was beyond him. Climb up? Use that white window stick to knock one down? But before he could decide, the hall door rattled as Mr Carter backed up against it, talking to someone.

Kevan closed the door on himself and stood in the dark, his breath ragged in the musty air. Mr Carter entered, and a *clonk* followed as he put his lunch on his desk. He sat heavily in his chair and sighed.

Kevan opened the door just a crack: Mr Carter in profile, his hands on the edge of his desk, sitting in silence for what seemed like forever, before slowly forking some Chicken Supreme into his mouth.

Then a knock. The door from the corridor opened; Kevan closed his. A *clink* and another sigh from Mr Carter: 'Come in, why don't you?'

Kevan checked his watch with the light – 13:34. He literally didn't have time for this.

'What happened to you? How can you get covered in mud so quickly? And where did the mud even come from?'

The boy was mumbling, but Kevan could just about hear something about pronouncing words for the presentation. It was his voice that struck Kevan. He couldn't place it – a bit whiny, a bit slow.

'Ah I see,' Mr Carter said. 'Yes, fair enough – you lot didn't know you were reading it out, I suppose. Let me get a textbook.'

His desk drawer began to open. Kevan's face cooled in the blackness. He'd left the key in the door, and Mr Carter was going to see it. A little rustling on the desk – Mr Carter still searching. Soon Kevan would be discovered.

'Oh, you've got one there. Okay, let's see then.' The rattly rumble of the blackboard being rolled up to a clear section.

Kevan opened the door again – Mr Carter was now stood side-on to the blackboard, his back to Kevan. Kevan couldn't see the boy, but he saw the textbook on the desk.

'So, this is "Anthracite". "An-thra-cite". My goodness, boy, are you okay? Have you been ill?'

Kevan stepped out, crept across the classroom, and as the two faced the board, he took the textbook and backed away, toward the hall door, flinching in fear that Mr Carter would reach again for the textbook.

Mrs Wells was back in position at the main entrance, so Kevan held his book to his side and walked confidently past her into the playground. He ran down the side of the building to the steps.

Anish wasn't there. Just his rucksack, limp on the wet gravel.

Kevan came back out to the main playground, turning, scanning, coming up short, as thunder began to breach the eastern valley ridge far behind the school.

He got back to the dinner hall but Anish wasn't there either.

13:39. This was it – he only had twenty-one minutes of lunch to get this done. Forget about Anish; just find the page

34

about Valley Hill coal and copy, word-for-word. Bad homework was better than no homework.

The hall was half-empty and most of the teachers had gone, so Kevan dumped his rucksack, sat at the end of a row of tables and opened the book to the Contents page. Chapter 2: Valley Hill Coal. Page 11.

'What you doing here? Finished snogging your boyfriend round the steps?' Ya-Ya stood over him, his grin full of mischief.

'Leave me alone, Ya-Ya,' Kevan said, knowing that he wouldn't. In fact, he sat opposite and spun the textbook a half-turn.

'You doing your homework? Now? But you said you'd done it. Does Mr Carter know about this?' Ya-Ya inquired, loudly, looking around.

Kevan yanked the book back.

'Shut up!'

'There's no need to be like that. Where's Anish? Why isn't he helping you? Isn't that what boyfriends are supposed to do?'

Kevan took a deep breath and stood, with the textbook gripped against his chest. He didn't even know where he was going – just away. But Ya-Ya kept stepping in front of him and reaching for his textbook.

'I can help, Kev. I've done my homework.

'Why won't you let me help?

'I'm just trying to help.'

It was all over and Kevan knew it. He pushed Ya-Ya, who fell against a table, and it screeched sharply. Heads turned.

'Shut up you – you bloody… fluckstake!' Kevan yelled.

The canteen darkened, as if thick clouds had passed over the windows. No-one spoke. Kevan's vision narrowed to just

Ya-Ya, and his red face, and his pointy grin. And then a clear, deep voice cut through the fog:

'You two. In here. Now.'

Kevan turned and walked slowly past Mr Carter, following Ya-Ya into the classroom, swallowing hard.

# Chapter 5

The rain hammered Valley Hill, the roads and rooves spectral with white spray, the gutters overwhelmed by torrents. Cars hissed by, the brake lights turning from deep ruby to primary red at the approach to each puddle. Kevan felt the Action Slip in his pocket as he hunched into his coat and stomped down the Old West Road toward home, seeming to find every loose paving stone, which sploshed underfoot.

After being done by Mr Carter, he'd then had to sit through a parade of goody-two-shoeses reading out their homework for Mr Protheroe, who wiped his eyes and clapped loudly for each, no matter how rubbish it was. If anyone had written about the disaster, then Mr Carter hadn't chosen them to read it out. Instead, there was a reading about headstocks and wheels, about lamps, about flipping coal seams.

Anish had sat there, quiet as a mouse – probably feeling bad for going AWOL. At times Kevan couldn't watch the presentations, and gazed out of the window; at one point between readings he'd found himself distracted by a sodden passerby, stood across the road. Gazing through the playground railings at their red, creased, miserable face, Kevan mused that, aside from their comparative wetness, it was like looking in a distant mirror.

And then he felt the presence of someone behind him. He saw the hem of the suit jacket, that weird, shiny, tweedy material, worn by Mr Protheroe.

'You appear to be elsewhere,' he'd said, kindly. But Mr Carter's expression as he stood, arms folded near the blackboard, didn't echo that kindness.

The rain had eased by afternoon break and while the rest of the class ran out, Mr Carter had given Kevan lines on the blackboard – "I will not hurt others, verbally or otherwise" – twenty times. When he'd finished the third line, Kevan asked Mr Carter what the Action Slip was actually for. Just out of curiosity. Just for the record.

Mr Carter gestured to the lines on the board.

'Well, it was a triple-whammy, wasn't it, Master Bevan. Lying, pushing, swearing.'

'But I said "Fluckstake", which isn't a swear word.'

'What is a "Fluckstake"?'

'I don't know.'

Mr Carter sat back.

'But you preceded it with "Bl"– with the "B" word. Which most certainly is one. So, you'd combined your last three transgressions into one neat little bundle. And the cherry on top – no homework.'

Kevan had asked whether he'd have still got an Action Slip if it was just the homework thing. Mr Carter stood there, much like when he was looking at the chair carnage from the previous day.

'We'll never know, will we, Master Bevan.'

Before home-time Mr Protheroe talked and talked and talked. About the museum, about the visitor's centre, about the national and local strikes. He said nothing about the disaster, apart from that some of the terraces nearby had become 'uninhabitable'.

'Not that they were particularly homely in the first place!' he'd said, jovially.

'I guess they don't compare with your big mine owner's house, Mr Protheroe,' Mr Carter had said, his arms still folded.

'Well, if your dream home is one with rising damp and subsidence, I suppose not,' Mr Protheroe said.

'And the land you sold to the big supermarket – were all the houses on there uninhabitable?'

Mr Protheroe continued to smile, and turned to Mr Carter.

'Yes. Most of them.'

'Well, I'm sure the small business owners in the town will welcome a bit of competition from a large national chain.'

'Anything that stops people leaving Valley Hill to do their shopping, Mr Carter.'

The bell couldn't have interrupted this dull and unnecessarily tense exchange soon enough, until Kevan remembered what was in store for him at home. And his travelling companion didn't make it any easier.

Anish didn't even crack a smile when Kevan made light of the Action Slip on the way home, which grated, because his wingman had baled on him. And when Kevan said 'what happened to you at lunchtime?', Anish shot him a look he'd never seen from him before – astonishment that darkened into rage – barked out 'Ya-Ya – oh!' threw up his hands and stalked up the path to his front door.

Sounded like Ya-Ya had got to him too.

The rain almost roared up from the ground as thunder rolled around the valley, and lightning sharpened the western ridgeline. Kevan turned onto Meifod Crescent and mentally updated his "To Do" list:

- Don't do homework – done. Or, not done.
- Lie, fight and swear – done.
- Get done by Mr Carter – done.
- Fall out with Anish – done.
- Get grounded, miss Wrestlemania, have Wrestlemania ruined – pending.

Kevan opened the gate and sloped down the path to the door. Maybe if he started crying, and came in like that? Like he was already sorry for what happened? Well, he *was* sorry, and the lump in his throat was proof.

"Donald Where's Your Trousers?" was on the kitchen radio, and he could see the murky silhouette of Dad in the kitchen, doing some kind of Highland jig. Why do parents have to be in a good mood just before you let them down?

He leant his hand against the inner door as he wiped his shoes on the "Wellcome" mat.

If only he could go back and do the homework; just one day.

'I wish I could go back in time,' he mumbled, tears welling in his eyes as the rain rat-a-tat-tatted on the porch roof. 'I wish I could go back in time, just one day.' He stomped onto the mat and scraped his shoes back, brushing a sleeve across his eyes. 'Just – one –'

Lightning and thunder struck at once, but almost like it was in the porch. Or even, inside his body. Kevan blinked but the tears were gone. He turned toward the porch windows. They were steamed up, but he could tell even before he wiped one with his sleeve that the sky was blue – the storm had passed. How long had he been in the porch?

From his side-lit reflection in the window, he could see his hair was thick and tall, like a hedge on his head. How did that happen?

Perhaps the whole porch had been hit by lightning. Maybe Mam would take pity on him if he'd been electrocuted?

Nah – even if he was burnt to a crisp, he'd still get grounded.

He opened the door slowly and stepped into the hall. "Back to Life" was playing again.

Dad popped his head round the kitchen door and wiggled his moustache. He was wrapping his hand in a wet JayCloth. Were his fingers still hurting? He really should go to the hospital.

'You okay pal?'

Kevan could smell charcoal. He moved toward the kitchen.

'Isn't it Chicken Surprise tonight?' he mumbled, almost to himself.

Mam's exasperated voice came from the pantry:

'No, Kevan, that's tomorrow.'

'You've got a whole day to wait for that particular feast,' Dad said.

They'd never had barbecue twice in a row, but it didn't surprise him that Dad had burnt his fingers again.

Kevan steeled himself, took a breath, and opened his mouth to confess.

'I said go wash your hands!' Mam yelled from the pantry. 'I won't ask you again.'

He shook his head. Gaw, she was like a stuck record sometimes. He moved to the foot of the stairs and began to climb, but froze when he heard a voice come from his bedroom:

'Okay, Okay! I'm going.'

Kevan ducked; someone stomped out of his bedroom and into the bathroom. The water ran briefly, before the footsteps returned to his room.

Kevan slowly climbed the remaining stairs, and peered through the banister spindles.

Some kid was in his room playing *Metroid*. He was even fighting the dinosaur-alien – how did he get hold of the passcodes?

Kevan approached the bedroom doorway. He was about to yell 'Oi' – the best he could do at short notice – when he examined the boy from behind, and began to quietly inhale until his lungs were set to burst.

Maroon Sweater – Valley Hill Primary.

Blue exercise book – Seven Carter.

Elasticated tie, skewiff on his collar –

Greasy hair –

Overweight –

Kevan sidestepped into the bathroom and climbed into the bath. He leant over to the sill and grabbed his can of Lynx Oriental deodorant, pulled the shower curtain across, and crouched low. He popped the top off the Lynx, shook it and aimed it at the curtain.

He could hear the boy bashing his buttons, and the occasional *bleep* and *bloop* from the games console. Shortly there was a *thud-thud-thud* down the stairs, and Kevan found a moment to breathe a little smoother.

He put the Lynx down and stayed still. Soon, voices came to him from the garden, via the bumpy pane of the bathroom window. Kevan slowly moved Dad's Brut 33 and pulled the window lever off the peg. He pushed; the window finally gave with a muted honk.

Kevan inched forward to peer through the gap. First it was the neighbour's shed, then the side of Dad's head. And finally, discussing supermarket sausages with Dad was the boy from upstairs. The boy he'd nearly yelled at.

It was him.

Kevan Bevan.

Did he really sound that whiny?

# Chapter 6

Kevan gripped the bathrail to ease the ache in his legs from the crouching.

'Okay,' he gasped. 'Okay. This is crazy. So – I've somehow travelled back in time. Okay. And I've nearly met myself. That's fine! And I've nearly wet myself. Not great. And now… I'm hiding in the bath.

'Just breathe. Just for a minute. Take it in.'

He looked around the bathroom. He'd been in here a lot in his life, but it seemed like someone else's bathroom, as if the layout, the colour, was unfamiliar.

He could hear Mam below the window, teasing Dad on his summer getup while the other Kevan – Kevan #1, he supposed, given that *he* was the original – played with Fenwick. The family was fractured into colourful blobs by the bumpy contours of the bathroom window pane.

The strange thing was, he didn't feel like he had travelled through time. It was more like the world had gone back in time around him. He was no different, but the world, the people, seemed to be on some kind of warped repeat. He'd been at his Bristol cousins' house once and, during a summer barbecue, they played "Rapper's Delight"; but while the rapping was the same, the background music was completely different from what Kevan had heard before. He was told it was a 'remix'. This felt like that – like everyone was doing the same thing but from a different angle.

Kevan had to get out of the house, and he had to do it now, because Mam would be coming back in soon, and then he'd be trapped upstairs. And who knew what would happen if he was discovered? A rip through time-space, or a black hole would appear in the hallway and suck the entire valley into it. And if not that, then everyone would at the very least be pretty confused.

Running away wasn't exactly a strategy, but what else could he do?

Well, he could freak Mam and Dad out. That would be fun for a moment before the Universe disappeared up its own jacksie.

He could take Kevan #1 to one side and explain the situation. As long as the Universe remained intact then they could have all sorts of fun – they could take it in turns, going to school while the other played computer games. They could play tricks on people. Bit of a risk – the whole Universe against a few practical jokes. It tipped slightly in favour of the Universe.

Or he could kill Kevan #1. Because if he didn't, then he would have to sleep rough. Out in the street, in the rain, while that impostor played *Metroid* on his console. Forever. He'd be homeless, miserable, starving to death, while this other Kevan would eat *his* crisps, play *his* games, go to *his* school–

Hold on. That's not right.

Kevan realised something. If you go back to the past, you can kind of see into the future.

He knew what Kevan #1 would do because he had already done it the day before. Kevan #1 would go to bed, get up, go to school, get an Action Slip, come home and then disappear into the past. All Kevan had to do was wait it out overnight, somewhere safe, and not change anything. The

45

woods past the cul-de-sac would do it. It wouldn't rain until early tomorrow morning. Then he could amuse himself until later in the afternoon, and reappear after #1 disappeared into the past. Into today. Back to today.

This was getting confusing pretty quick.

He stood and his legs gave way. He gripped the shower curtain and swung slightly onto the bath edge, where he sat heavily.

Try again.

He shouldered his rucksack and started down the stairs, reaching the porch door. And then he stopped.

This was where it happened. This was where he'd travelled back in time. He was blubbing and praying and begging, and it just happened. Maybe he could try going back to Friday. But how?

He could give blubbing another go. Maybe that activated the... thing. Or was it the lightning? Could that send you through time? It did in *Back To The Future*. Well, there was no lightning now. Hopefully it was the blubbing. Then he wouldn't have to hide in a tree.

He had just enough time before Mam came back in. He opened the door and stood in the porch. He rubbed his hands together and bent his knees – as if he was going to do a ski jump, like Eddie The Eagle – and closed his eyes tight.

'I wish I could go back to my own time. Friday! Yes, Friday! The thirtieth. Of March. Nineteen-ninety. I want to go back to Friday the thirtieth of March, nineteen-ninety.'

He screwed his eyes tighter.

'Around four o'clock.'

He peered out of one eye, then shut it tight again.

'In the afternoon!'

He opened his eyes: nothing. He ran his hand through his hair, blinking in exasperation, and looked out at the blue sky. Maybe he *did* need thunder and lightning.

And then Fenwick barked.

Kevan stayed absolutely still. If he didn't move, perhaps Fenwick–

Nope. He heard the dog scratching across the kitchen lino, and there he was, in the hallway, eyeing Kevan through the porch door, and although Kevan was closing it, he was still trying to do it slow so that no-one heard, and the dog's muzzle was in the gap before he could click it shut.

Kevan hissed at him.

'Fenwick! No! Stobbit!'

He managed to push Fen's nose out and close the inner door. He looked through the greyed netting at the dog. Fenwick looked toward the kitchen, then back to Kevan, his eyes shining.

'I'm sorry,' Kevan whispered. 'You've had a lot to deal with today, haven't y–'

Kevan looked up. Kevan #1 was stood by the back door. And he was looking right through the kitchen, down the hallway, at him. He couldn't breathe – #1 just stood there, staring. It was like a mirror, but flipped; #1 looked the wrong way round. His parting was on the other side and one eyebrow looked higher than the other.

'What is it, boy?' Kevan #1 said as he came into the kitchen. Kevan realised #1 wasn't looking at him – he was looking at Fenwick.

'For god's sake, Andrew – I told you I don't want to go to that big supermarket.'

#1 turned and went back out to the garden.    Fenwick hesitated, then turned and began to pad away, occasionally looking back.

Kevan breathed, his heart pounding.

One last try. He stood on the mat and closed his eyes.

'I wish it was tomorrow.'

Nothing.

'I really wish it was tomorrow.'

Still nothing.

'No – I said "just one day".'

He cleared his throat and addressed the inner porch door.

'I wish I could go forward in time, just one day.'

Nothing.

He tried to think back. Exactly what was he doing? He was stood on the mat – no – he was wiping his feet. Maybe that charged up the porch, like pedalling on Dad's bike powered the light.

He started wiping his feet.

'I wish I could go forward in time, just one day.'

Again, nothing.

Then he heard voices out the back: 'No I'm fine – I'm just cold.'

It was Mam. She was coming back in.

Kevan started wiping his feet faster. He hissed at the door.

'I wish I could go forward in time, just one day.'

Mam came into the kitchen and flopped her magazine onto the table. She muttered 'blimming *Marsdens*' before getting a glass and going to the sink.

'Oh please, oh please!' Kevan whispered. 'I wish I could go forward just one day.'

He could see her back and heard the cold tap. He carried on wiping his feet, sweat forming on his brow. The cold tap stopped – Mam picked up her magazine. He had one more chance before he was busted.

48

'I wish–'

There was a flash and a sudden wall of sound, like the white noise on his telly, before Kevan realised it was the rain, once again hammering the porch roof. He looked back down the darkened hallway. Dad was trying to do 'The Worm' to that song about Magic Number Three.

Kevan opened the door and sniffed.

'Chicken Surprise! Yes!' He punched the air.

Dad stopped and looked at Kevan, puzzled and amused. Mam peeked round the doorframe, before whipping Dad with the tea towel.

'Ow!'

'Did you put him up to that?'

Dad emitted a confused laugh: 'It wasn't me.'

'Wipe your feet,' she said to Kevan.

'Okay, yeah, okay.'

Kevan leapt into the porch and closed the inner door. He started wiping his feet, but felt a rustle in his pocket and pulled out the Action Slip. He turned it over in his hand, remembered everything that that little rectangle of paper meant. Humiliation. Grounding. No Wrestlemania.

'Chicken Surprise is going to have to wait,' he said to himself. 'I've got homework to do.'

He continued wiping his feet, faster and faster, screwed his eyes shut, and whispered to the door.

# Chapter 7

Night began to settle the house. Mam and Dad talked for a bit, with the telly on low, then Mam went to bed while Dad promptly snored in his chair, later to be startled out of it by Patrick Moore on *The Sky At Night*. He pottered about the living room and kitchen, getting another beer from the fridge – his third! – before necking it and climbing the stairs. A few creaks of their bed and all was quiet.

Kevan's legs cramped so much he had to bite his finger not to scream. He knew the understairs cupboard lost space to the pantry on the other side but still he had clambered into it – while Dad and Kevan #1 were in the garden – not reckoning with the board games and Christmas decorations with which he had to share space all evening. He'd wanted to wait at least an hour from Dad's first snore, but it wasn't to be – he rolled out onto the carpet at the sound of the first guttural growl from upstairs, kicked his leg out and gasped quietly.

The cool draught along the hallway floor brought blessed relief. He lit his Casio watch: 0:45:17 SA 3-31. But it wasn't quarter to one in the morning on Saturday 31st March anymore – it was that time, but Friday the 30th. He pressed one of the buttons and the "12" flashed, pressed again until the minutes flashed, then the seconds, then the day. He was about to change it when there was a gentle chink from the pantry; Fenwick stirring. Kevan lowered his arms and lay still, the moonlight gleaming off the hallway lampshade. A contented fart from the dog; Kevan rolled over slowly and raised himself up.

Showtime.

As Dad had demonstrated on the stairs above him about 20 minutes ago, every step had suddenly developed a creak. Not just the first and sixth; now it was all of them, and no matter where Kevan placed his feet, each one called out, like a frog, croaking 'Waa-aake'.

He kept having to remember to breathe, and his heart thumped high up near his throat as he neared the landing.

This was it: no going back.

But first he needed a wee.

A dim blue-white glow came from the bathroom – moonlight fractured through frosted glass. The lino seemed really hard and echoey, and while the moonlight at least helped him aim, he still splashed a bit. He dared not flush.

He got to his bedroom door and placed a hand on the knob. He waited for a long rumble from Dad's snore before he turned it, opened the door slowly and crept in.

Kevan #1 had left the computer on, with *Metroid* paused, and even though it was mainly black, with just Samus stood there, paused on a platform, the screen gave off a ghostly glow, lighting up the edges of furniture, gleaming off the wardrobe handles.

Kevan stood there, his every muscle taut, his heartbeat now in his head, making it throb and pulse while sweat stuck his school shirt to his back. He'd planned to wait for his night vision to improve so that he could move around easier, hoping that the room would still be dark enough that he didn't see #1 in bed, but now he felt exposed, trapped by the light.

It was better if he just thought there was someone else in his bed, rather than himself from a day ago. He stared ahead

51

at the far wall and took a step into the bedroom – all of the brass wardrobe handles rattled. Kevan glanced sharply at the bed and gasped.

And there was Kevan #1 – *him* – out for the count, the glistening line of drool from his mouth to the pillow clearly visible thanks to the glow from the screen.

It was shocking. It was like an out-of-body experience, but instead of hovering above, Kevan was just cemented to the carpet. That was him, last night, now.

He shook his head vigorously, crept slowly round to #1's rucksack by the wardrobe and gingerly unzipped it. He felt inside: the hardback textbook was under about five magazines.

But why couldn't he find it Friday lunchtime? Maybe it had been there all along and he'd just panicked. It was getting too confusing. He had to stick to the plan; he just needed it for a few hours and then he'd replace it.

He couldn't find his exercise book. Perhaps – yes, down by the far side of the bed, near Fuzwuz and Marjorie Donk. He half-squatted, half-waddled over and picked it up.

He couldn't leave the game on. If Mam came in next morning she'd be well annoyed to see that he'd been playing late into the night. He reached over to the console to switch it off, vaguely aware in the back of his mind that Mam hadn't been annoyed, because she hadn't come in, while also thinking dully that he should turn the TV off first, because–

Suddenly the white noise blasted harshly through the room, lighting up Kevan #1, before Kevan twisted the on/off/volume knob on TV.

Silence. Pitch black. The sweat began to push hotly out of his skin. He heard Kevan #1 stirring, but as long as Kevan stayed still there was no reason–

Mam and Dad's bedroom door creaked open, and Dad padded across the landing. Light from the bathroom beamed under both the door and Kevan's bed. Kevan lay on the damp carpet and listened to wee thundering into the bowl.

The bedsprings groaned above. Kevan froze. A wisp of air on his cheek; Kevan #1 had turned and their faces were now inches apart, #1's breath shallow and warm, still clutching One-eyed Colin, whereas Kevan's breath was ragged, and he was still gripping his book.

Then the toilet flushed, and the pipes roared through the walls as the cistern filled up again. #1 opened his eyes slightly – a pinprick of light in each. Kevan froze again – his head began to ache and he felt dizzy. #1 began to whimper – he turned in his bed and began to thrash slowly. The whimper became a long moan. Kevan stood sharply. The light under the door flickered and jostled with shadow – Dad was stood outside.

Kevan snuck to the wall by the door, ignoring the *clack-a-clack* of the wardrobe handles, and held his breath as the door opened slowly and a strip of light draped over the bed.

Kevan #1 stirred again, but the moan was back to a whimper. And then Dad's voice from the landing:

'You okay, pal?'

'Yeah,' Kevan said from behind the door, and clamped a hand over his own mouth. He gazed at #1, who curled up and made a contented grunt.

'Get back to sleep boy,' Dad said softly, and the door closed. Then the bathroom light went out and the darkness fell onto Kevan, closer and deeper than before. He stood there, rigid, until the house settled once more.

Every step creaked with gusto on the way down too.

He still needed paper but thanks to Mam's nag from earlier – from a few hours in the *future* – he knew where to get it: Dad's clipboard. He padded over to the bureau in the dining bit and reached into his case. There were about fifty sheets on top of some kind of quality control forms, in a thin triplicate of white, yellow and pink, and all were clipped fast to a hard vinyl rectangular board. He took it out and was about to unclip the paper when he heard panting.

Fenwick's big head was visible beyond the dining table, raised up from his basket in the pantry. Kevan took a breath and walked slowly over.

'Fen my boy, it's just me, it's just Kev.' Kevan held out his hand; Fenwick warily placed his muzzle into his palm for the briefest of moments. He seemed to be satisfied.

★

Fenwick's big barrel chest rose and fell slowly, as Kevan lay down on the pantry floor and nuzzled the back of his head into the Labrador's warm, golden fur. He brought his legs up, planted his feet on the kitchen lino and rested the clipboard on his lap. The pantry bulb initially shone harshly into the hallway, but he'd closed the accordion door thing, figuring that the squeaking and scraping as it unfolded was worth it to blot the light out.

He had to focus on the homework – if he gave himself a moment to think about what had happened, with all the time travel and stuff, he'd get tied up in knots. This wasn't like *Bill & Ted's Excellent Adventure*, or *Back To The Future*; he was tired and hungry, and unlike the heroes of those films, he had to avoid his past self. And help his past self. Both, at the same time.

'That's the only thing I haven't quite worked out, Fen,' he murmured, stuffing a Kit Kat wrapper into his pocket. 'How do I get the homework to me – to #1? Do it now and

54

sneak it into his rucksack? Leave a note on it to make sure he looks before setting off to school? Sign it "A Friend"?'

For the third time, he wrote the date on the top line. He had to pull the sheet out and start again when he realised he'd put Saturday 31st March 1990. He really needed to update his watch. On the next sheet – attempt #4 – he chose Wednesday 28th March 1990, two days before it was due. Why not? It would look like he was organised, and Mr Carter would feel stupid for assuming on Thursday that he hadn't done it. And then he decided that he wasn't just going to hand any old rubbish in; if Kevan #1 was going to have to read it out loud, it had better be a masterpiece. The look on Mr Carter's face when Kevan read something out that was half-decent would be priceless. You want some homework? How about some *brilliant* homework?

That'll show him.

'Thing is, Fen, I wouldn't have a problem writing about Granddad, and the explosion. But how can I fit it on one side of A4? "Granddad was a miner at Valley Hill Colliery, but he got blown up and then Mam and Gran were evicted, and then they moved in with Jackie and her mam and dad, and then my Mam met my Dad, and then Gran moved out of Bumptown." Bit short, isn't it?'

He opened the textbook to have a skim read. There were five black-and-white photos of black lumps, with a word under each. He recognised one of the words.

'An-thra-cite,' he read, breaking it down like Mr Carter did to that boy. At least two of the other words he couldn't pronounce. Never mind – like Mr Carter said, none of them knew they were reading it out.

'"For many years a debate raged as to whether Valley Hill coal should be classed as high-grade Anthracite or be given its own classification due to its superior qualities."'

Kevan snorted. '"Raged". Well, this is a thriller and no mistake, eh, Fen?'

Fenwick let out a long, low snore.

'Quitter,' Kevan said, shaking his head. Although he didn't blame him. It was cosy down here, with a cool draught and a warm dog. He stifled a yawn as Fen's chest rose slowly up and down.

Thumping steps descending the stairs above the pantry announced the morning. Kevan's heart thumped too – he opened his eyes and checked his watch – 7:10. He looked at the clipboard. Just the date – again.

# Chapter 8

The inner porch door opened and closed; Mam getting the milk. Fenwick padded over and sniffed at the accordion door – it was never closed, but it gave Kevan a moment to slide the clipboard into his bag. Putting the rucksack on would create too much noise; he had to leave it there and skirt across and into the dining bit near the bureau.

'What the ...?' Mam murmured to the accordion door. Kevan moved into the living room as she pulled it open and entered the kitchen.

The ground floor worked a bit like a loop – in through the front door, down the hall, into the kitchen, right into the dining bit, right, into the living room, right, again, through the door into the hall. You could walk laps of it, if you dodged the kitchen table. As long as he could hear Mam, he would have a chance of staying ahead of her enough so that she wouldn't see him.

Mam put the kettle on and bustled. She was moving around too much for Kevan to dart to the front door, and besides which his rucksack was still in the pantry, so he stayed in the living room.

'Oh, that boy,' she whispered.

Her slippered footsteps entered the hallway. She dropped something by the coats and returned to the kitchen. Kevan peered through the doorway – it was his rucksack. Now he just needed her to stop busying.

On cue – silence. Kevan peeked back into the kitchen. Mam was sat at the table with a cup of tea, her dressing-gowned back to him. Now was his chance.

But he hesitated.

What was she doing?

She was just sitting there. Not reading, not sipping her tea, not listening to the radio. Maybe she'd fallen asleep. But no – she ran a hand through her hair and ruffled it. This might be harder than when she was ranging around the kitchen. At least then she was distracted; at least then, there was noise.

And then he heard it. Quietly at first, but definitely something.

Mam was whispering to herself.

Kevan could have snuck out ten times over by now – although with the lack of general noise in the kitchen it would have still been a challenge – but he needed to know what she was saying. Probably something about his homework.

Kevan talked to himself too. Sometimes it was to the posters, sometimes in bed, with One-Eyed Colin. But mainly it was just to himself. He would rehearse devastating responses to imagined arguments with Ya-Ya, or witty, cool statements to impress Gwen. Sometimes, he would work himself up into a frenzy over some comment at school, or if someone teased him about his weight, or how poor they were.

But he'd never heard Mam do it.

The whispers got louder, but stayed whispers. Kevan was able to make out some of the words. It was like a chant, or some kind of Mr Motivator stuff.

'Come on, girl. Just another day. Just get them up, make breakfast, send them off. Just another day. One thing at a time.'

Kevan frowned. Mam just sat there, gibbering away while steam curled from her tea.

'Give Jackie a call. Why not? Nothing to stop me just popping over, even. Say hello, cup of tea, straight back. Nothing to it.'

He regretted hanging around – her whispers were dull as dishwater. He crept into the hall toward his rucksack, but then there was thudding above his head. Dad was up, and he was coming down.

Kevan glanced quickly into the kitchen: Mam stood, rubbed her eyes, and went to the side, obscured by the pantry; then the noise of cereal tinkling into a bowl and Paula Abdul on the radio.

He could use the ground floor 'loop' but only as long as everyone moved in the same direction, which never happened. So he pressed himself against the side of the stairs, hoping Dad would breeze into the living room.

Dad clumped down the stairs and into the hallway.

'Morning pal,' he said, as he did some joke body blows and patted him on the cheek before entering the kitchen.

This was Kevan's chance. He moved toward the front door.

More steps downstairs: Kevan #1. And he knew that #1 went straight to the kitchen.

Pantry? No – he'd be trapped. Both Mam and Dad's backs were turned so he scrambled under the kitchen table, clattering into the chairs; both parents vaguely admonished the dog in unison, and Fenwick's ears pricked in confusion from the basket.

Kevan could see his family's feet and sometimes legs moving around the table, turning, shuffling as they talked. This, he realised too late, was no better than the pantry.

Finally, a chair scraped out and Kevan #1 sat down. Kevan inched away from his legs, but they swung out and a shin caught him on the jaw.

'Soz Fen,' Kevan #1 mumbled.

Dad clumped back into the kitchen, hissing under his breath. Then Mam went to the cupboard. There then followed the exchange about Kit Kats and clipboards. Kevan felt the Kit Kat wrapper in his pocket as he peered at the rucksack by the front door, a corner of the clipboard just poking out of the zip. Mam's feet flicked into view as she and Dad did their ragdoll routine. Then the conversation about Wrestlemania and mud. Then Mam made Dad sit down and have some breakfast – toast with jam – while Kevan #1 sloped off upstairs.

That toast smelled good though. Fenwick must have been thinking the same thing because his head rose slightly, plaintive in his basket. Kevan looked round; Dad was holding half a slice of toast under the table, waggling it.

Then he tapped Kevan with his boot and waggled the toast again.

In a normal situation Kevan wouldn't allow himself to be fed like a dog – even the Bevans had more dignity than that – but this was not a normal situation, and Kevan had had one Kit Kat since yesterday lunchtime. He shrugged at Fenwick. He reached out to take the toast, thought twice, then nosed it, and ate it out of Dad's hand. Dad patted him once on the head before Kevan quickly moved away. Fenwick barked. Dad told him to quieten down, perhaps too tired to question who he'd just fed if Fen was in his basket.

'So… what are you up to today?' Dad said.

'Oh. I dunno,' Mam said.

Dad's legs opened and closed. 'How about you go see Jackie?'

'Yeah, maybe,' Mam said, clearly irritated.

Jackie was Mam's best mate from way back. It was her family that Mam and Gran moved in with after the disaster. "Aunt Jackie", but not really an Aunt. She was all bangles and bracelets, long white teeth and big pink gums, loud voice, found everything hilarious, everything exciting, everything interesting.

Dad's legs jogged under the table.

'Look, I'm not pushing. It just might do you some good to get out of the house for a bit.'

'I'm not a patient, Andrew.'

'I know. I know. But if you're not busy–'

Mam's feet turned in Dad's direction.

'What?'

'Well…' Dad's legs squeezed together. '…perhaps you should be.'

There was a brief silence before Mam responded.

'I will go see Jackie.'

'Good.'

'When I'm ready.'

Dad's legs sagged apart.

'Okay, love.'

He pushed his chair back and stood.

'…where *is* that flippin' clipboard?'

The table was now clear – Dad was back in the lounge, looking around the chairs and settee by the sounds of things. Kevan inched out and stood, his back cricking like an old man's. If Kevan #1 was upstairs, he could simply blag his way out. And to be honest, he was fed up with sneaking around.

He marched to the front door and picked up his rucksack.

'Bye then!' Mam said.

Kevan peered up the stairs, smiled at Mam in the kitchen, then waved.

# Chapter 9

It rained hard, the distant valley ridgelines surrounding Bumptown shrouded in layers of lightening grey until they blended into the sky. This time round however, Kevan wasn't meeting Anish, so he picked up his BMX and began to pedal down the middle of the street. He looked at his watch – 8:25. He didn't quite know where he was going, but if he was going to get this homework done, he needed a roof.

He rode across Old West Road and a Ford Fiesta screeched to a halt, fishtailing slightly. It beeped, the driver's face as red as the car. Kevan stopped for a moment. Was that the car that splashed them by the adventure playground? He was sure it was. It *certainly* was.

Kevan made a gesture with his fist and his arm and cycled on, and the driver responded by revving and accelerating off, his tyres juddering on the slick tarmac.

Sometimes Anish would stand at the living room window, waiting for Kevan to turn up at his garden gate and yell for him, so he kept his head low and accelerated past.

The pirate's cabin at the adventure playground wasn't really made for people his age or size. He put his bike behind a bush, up the handholds, across the rope bridge, and wedged himself in at the captain's table, making sure to avoid the weird bluey-green blob stuck on the bench. He got the clipboard out of his bag,

Despite all the space-time continuum stuff, he was going to march up to #1, stuff the homework in his hand and march away without saying a word. He knew himself; #1 wouldn't care too much how it had happened – he would leave those questions to Anish. Besides, Kevan had come up with a way to avoid the whole Universe exploding thing: he would wear his coat backwards and put his hood up over his face. Then he would just be a kindly, faceless stranger.

Kevan wasn't actually sure what time he and Anish usually got to the adventure playground to cross the fields; if they had already passed by, he would have to catch up with them. If not, he would try to intercept. The homework was going to have to be a bodge – no masterpiece for #1.

He wrote "There are many types of coal."

'Oi, Bevan! What are you doing up there?'

It was Ya-Ya. He'd completely forgotten about this bit. Then he realised that he was the 'poor boy' who Ya-Ya was yelling up to. Which meant that #1 and Anish weren't far behind.

Kevan poked his head out of the small hatch at the side. Ya-Ya stood, looking up, while Hughesy rocked back and forth on the springy horse thing.

'Just leave me alone, Ya-Ya.'

'Where's Anish? Has he stood you up? I thought it was "Bev 'n' Dez 4 Eva"?'

Kevan cringed. Someone had seen it carved into one of the wooden posts in the adventure playground. Ever since then Ya-Ya had teased Kevan for being gay. He didn't even know who'd carved it – probably someone called Beverley and someone called Derek. Not that there was a single young person called Beverley or Derek in the whole of town.

A few more insults later and Ya-Ya moved off. Kevan wrote "Peat" and looked up sharply. Kevan #1 and Anish were crossing the road.

He bagged up his stuff and squirmed out of the cabin, swinging awkwardly off the monkey bars to get down.

He'd written four lines: Date, "Class Project", "Valley Hill Coal", and "There are many types of coal: Peat".

Change of plan – hide, wait for #1 and Anish to pass, get back in the cabin, finish, and then figure out how to get the homework to his past self before lunchtime.

He hid with his BMX behind the bush and peered out just in time to see #1 and Anish get sprayed by the passing car.

And it was a red Ford Fiesta.

He knew it. He knew it was the car. He felt a sense of vindication that he'd insulted the driver in the strongest possible terms if he was going to drive through puddles to soak children to the–

Hold on.

Perhaps the driver had done it because Kevan had insulted him. After all, Kevan's memory at that point was of the future, so he'd insulted the driver for something he hadn't done yet. And he might not have splashed them if Kevan hadn't insulted him.

Or maybe it was another Fiesta. There were plenty of red Fiestas around.

It gave him a headache just thinking about it. That dude from the Time Machine never had this trouble. He went to the future. And he was too busy saving entire races of people and snogging exotic women. Anish was much better at working out this kind of thing – if only this time-travel stuff had happened to him instead. He would have got *his* homework to Anish #1 already.

But then, Anish would have just done his homework in the first place.

Kevan heard a toddler mewling and looked out again from the bush; a rather peeved mother glared at Kevan while she helped her daughter into the cabin.

New plan: get homework done elsewhere, and get it to #1 during lunch.

Kevan grabbed his BMX and backed away, trying to keep the bushes between him and his past self. He kept moving until the playground was out of sight, and hid behind a crumbled wall between the fields and the garages at the back of some houses.

The track ran alongside the garages and fields until it reached the main road. The wall was about five feet high but it was partially collapsed in places so he was able to keep an eye on them both. Kevan #1 and Anish walked slowly across the fields. Anish occasionally looked at #1 as he gestured dramatically, his eyes wide. He looked like he'd been punched in the gut.

Speaking of gut, #1 – he – looked much fatter than he saw in the mirror. Perhaps it was the coat. Did everyone else really see him like that?

He didn't mind seeing himself in the mirror, but when he took his school shirt off to get changed and sat on his bed, his podge would push over his trousers, hiding his crotch. It was times like that that he hated himself. But then he wouldn't change his habits, so he couldn't quite understand how he could feel like that about himself and then just wolf more snacks.

He had tried to not eat so much but it was hard. There were always biscuits in the house, and once he'd eaten an entire packet.

And the biscuits were just a small part of it. There was the ice cream, the tinned peaches and pears, the Vienetta, the choc ices, the money for Scouts (the change from which he would spend on teddy bears or cola bottles from the corner shop, and eat until his stomach ached), and he would do the same thing all over again on a Saturday, if he didn't spend his pocket money in the Amusements.

Mam and Gran were no help either. If Gran wasn't encouraging him to have seconds, thirds and fourths, Mam was chiding him for cutting fat off his chops. Dad explained it once; something to do with the war, and rations, but it didn't make much sense.

The worst thing was Yorkshire Puddings. They didn't keep, Gran said, they had to be eaten, and she usually made 12 of them. Mam ate one; Gran had none or one; Dad usually struggled at four. That left six minimum for Kevan. And they were huge – puffed-up, light, crispy, and when you poured gravy into them–

On cue his tummy rumbled. He was starving. He'd only had a Kit Kat since lunch "yesterday". He had no money on him and he didn't know how to get any food.

He followed Kevan #1 and Anish to the main Westgate Road and watched them walk up. He kept one eye on the pavement for loose change, that someone may have dropped. He'd ask Kevan #1, but he knew his past self didn't have any money either.

Then nature called. He stood near some tall bushes and peed against the wall. He did a jiggle. Ha – it was funny, the idea of him cadging some money off his past self. He reached for his zip.

And then he stopped.

Of course! He could give himself money after all. But instead of using "past" him, he would get help from "future" him. Bill & Ted did it with Ted's dad's car keys in their *Excellent Adventure*. There was no reason why it wouldn't work for him.

He started looking around the ground, on walls, in little nooks and crannies, for some kind of random object that was there and – as far as he could tell – had been for a long time. Perhaps a rock, or some rag, or some litter.

Kevan stopped at a big yellow grit box. Wedged between it and the wall was an open beans tin, the label heavily faded. It had been there for as long as he could remember, unnoticed and, more importantly, unmoved.

After all of this homework business was over, Kevan Bevan swore that he was going to use the porch one more time to go back to before now – perhaps just earlier in the morning – to stash £1.50 of his pocket money in that can. If he kept his promise – and no one else had noticed it and pilfered it – there would be £1.50 in that can, right now.

He reached down.

And stopped.

What if there was no money in there?

What would that mean?

It would mean that for whatever reason he had been unable to get the money in there. Perhaps he had been unable to go back again. Well, that wouldn't be such a bad thing. After sorting out his homework, instead of leaping forward, he was just going to wait it out until later in the afternoon anyway. And then, apart from the money attempt, he wasn't doing it ever again anyway.

But what if it meant something else? What if something happened to him before, during or after travelling, so he couldn't leave himself the money? Something bad?

He shuddered.

Perhaps he shouldn't even check.

He stamped his foot in frustration. There might be £1.50 there just waiting, unclaimed, until someone else looked in there.

But if he checked and there was nothing there, he would fear the worst.

He took two steps.

His tummy rumbled.

Just don't overthink it. Bill & Ted didn't and they found the keys exactly where they planned to hide them.

He turned, reached into the gap and picked up the tin.

It was empty.

He groaned.

And for all his worrying about not being able to travel again, worrying about being stuck, worrying about being killed, worrying about worrying, he only groaned because he was just hungry.

# Chapter 10

Kevan crested the hill, bearing east, but instead of turning under the town gate arch on his left and onto the high street, he cycled on, until he saw the huge glass and brick superstore to his right: Marsdens.

Mr Carter once called it Valley Hill's new citadel, but Kevan wasn't sure what that meant. If citadels had vast car parks then Marsdens definitely was one.

Among other things, Dad said it had a café. Kevan was starving, and it would be hard to sit there with people eating and no money, but if it was anywhere near as big as Dad had described, he'd be able to sneak in there, find a table and get his homework done in no time. He had less chance of being recognised here than somewhere on the high street.

He leant his BMX against the wall near a cash machine and walked through the automatic doors, feigning confidence.

There was a big glass ceiling-type thing with a coin-op Noddy Car, then some more automatic doors, and then a row of shops within the shop, just like Dad said: a travel agent, a pharmacy, a HappySnaps, a dry cleaners. And at the far end, its warm yet pungent aroma of toast and bacon drawing him near, was the café.

There was a counter with a glass display for cakes and sausage rolls; behind it two people with uniforms and pinnies bustled. The seating bit had about twelve tables –

one table was taken up by big men in high-vis jackets but the others were empty.

It wasn't as massive as Dad made out. The ceilings were high but it was no bigger than Bumptown Munchtown (formerly Gatehouse Platehouse).

Kevan sat at the table furthest from the counter, and suddenly felt very exposed. He didn't know if he was being paranoid or whether people really were giving him the side-eye. Kevan #1 was at school this very moment, but that only meant the *school* thought he was there. To everyone else in Valley Hill, Kevan Bevan was skiving.

He slowly put his clipboard and textbook onto the table and began leafing through, looking for the coal page. A loud-voiced woman behind the counter for some reason made him hunch more. He got to the coal page as he heard a clatter of bangles, and he soon noticed an apron beyond the book; he raised the book slightly so that he didn't have to talk to the wearer. Because he knew. He knew who it was. He didn't want to be right about this, he'd come here because he didn't want to be recognised.

'What would you like, love?'

It was the word "love" that got him. The voice. The volume. The bangles. He lowered the book and looked up.

It was Jackie. Her eyes shone with mirth and affection. She pulled her sleeves back beyond her elbows, her bangles *click-clack*ing.

'Erm...' Kevan lifted a laminated menu from the table and began looking at it.

'Tell you what, I'll get you a glass of water while you look.'

Jackie walked off. Kevan wasn't sure whether he should bolt or wangle it. Although there wasn't much to wangle in this situation if you didn't have hard cash. But even if he left

71

now, Jackie had seen him in her café when he clearly should have been at school.

She came back and put a glass of water on the table. Kevan didn't realise how thirsty he was until he hesitantly put the glass to his lips – he downed it in five big gulps. He gasped and the water made his tummy rumble really loudly.

'Oh dear. Tell you what, I'll get you a scrambled egg on toast and you can pay me next time you're here.'

So… he was going to have to return to the supermarket at some point, with his own pocket money? It would have been free at home. But when he looked at Jackie again, she winked.

'Um… I don't know when I'll be back.'

'That's okay – no rush.' She winked again.

'Okay – how much is a scrambled egg on toast?'

'I'm not sure I've made myself–'

'And is the water free?'

'Yes, love,' and she said the next bit slowly and deliberately, 'Same as the scramble.' Then she did a really big wink.

'Oh,' he mumbled. 'It says £1.40.'

Jackie's face dropped and her voice went flat.

'I'm giving it you for free out of the kindness of my heart, Kevan.'

'Oh.' He laughed nervously. 'Okay.'

She leaned in.

'I saw you. Malcolm was driving me and I saw you. On the Main Westgate Road.'

Kevan frowned.

'You were looking in an old tin.'

'Oh.' And then the implication dawned: 'Oh.'

She smiled kindly and moved off.

'Auntie Jackie.'

She turned slowly.

'It's okay, love.'

He was about to call out again, tell her that he wasn't broke, they weren't broke, that if he knew he was going to a café he'd have brought his pocket money.

Because it was true – they weren't broke, no matter what Jackie thought, or Ya-Ya said. They were just skint. Dad once explained the difference: if you were skint, you'd turn the lights off around the house. If you were broke, the leccy company did it for you.

Surely Jackie already knew this? But then, Mam hadn't spoken to her in ages.

He decided not to protest. He was here now, and there was no going back. And he was famished.

Kevan looked at his book, couldn't concentrate on the text, put it down, hunched in himself to hide in plain sight. He felt like crying.

He saw a slightly wonky reflection of himself in the metal serviette holder. His hair was half-hedge, half matted. There was mud crusted in it, and on his forehead, and what looked like chocolate on the side of his mouth. His skin was red and blotchy, and he looked really tired. Because he *was* really tired.

A *cuh-clonk* and in front of him steamed a massive plate of scrambled egg, with two rounds of toast and a small lake of beans on one side. Jackie put down a tall red sauce bottle; Kevan flipped the top and squirted a big blob next to the eggs.

'You okay?'

Kevan looked up and nodded vigorously. She shifted onto her other hip.

'I know, I know. School's tough, isn't it?'

73

Kevan nodded as he forked a mound of scramble into his mouth. It was creamy and hot, just the way Mam made it.

'You know you can always talk to someone about it? Say, a teacher, or your Mammy and Daddy?'

Kevan blinked. He just wanted to eat his scramble. Mam did this too – putting his tea in front of him and then interrogate him about school. 'Mealtimes is our chance as a family to talk and spend time together,' she'd say. Yeah, if you wanted your food to go cold.

'Can you not talk to your Mammy and Daddy about it?'

Kevan shook his head. He couldn't, that was true. No one would believe him.

'Is there anything I can do, love?'

Kevan peered up at her. She looked concerned and a bit nervous. What was she talking about?

'Do you want *me* to talk to your Mam–'

Kevan pushed quickly away from the table. Jackie raised her hands.

'Okay, it's okay, I won't say anything. I just want to make sure you're safe. I remember Nathan at your age, and I'd hate to think–'

She glanced at the counter. A man in a shirt and tie was beckoning her over.

'You keep eating, love. I'll be right back.'

Kevan slowly came back to the table, picked up a slice of toast and started munching it, but didn't take his eyes off her, as she walked slowly back to the counter. The man began talking to her. He occasionally jerked his head in Kevan's direction. Kevan started eating quicker, as Jackie shrugged and opened her palms to him.

Soon the plate was clear. He stood up. Jackie was glaring at the man, while dramatically removing each bangle and placing them deliberately on the counter.

Kevan moved off, past the shops-in-a-shop, but there was a security guard stood in the window-y porch bit. Kevan turned, back past the shops, then entered the supermarket proper, the guard tailing him at a distance.

He walked to the far end until he reached the back counters. Dad was right – this place sold everything. Fresh bread, fresh fish, fresh meat. Maybe he should take Mam to this back bit. Although he couldn't see any socks.

The security guard took a turn down the main middle aisle as Kevan began skirting the counters – with each aisle he passed, the guard appeared and then disappeared, glaring at him all the while.

Soon he was going to run out of counters. If he got to the end, he would wait for the guard to start coming up the last aisle toward him, then run the other way–

Nope. Another guard was now slowly tailing him along the counters.

A-ha! A door. It said "Fire Exit", but so what? The "Girls" and "Boys" doors at school were fire exits, and though they were heavy, he could still open them.

This one had a metal bar. Even better – he pressed it down and the door opened easily.

And then a piercing shriek blasted above his head.

He ran, the guards and the alarm chasing him around the outside of the supermarket. Shortly he reached his bike, stepped on the pedal and pushed off, swinging his leg over and racing across the car park.

Chased by two security guards, setting off alarms, fleeing on his bike – and once again, Gwen Roberts wasn't there to see it.

# Chapter 11

He cycled on, along the Southgate Road, his head down, knowing the security guards weren't sprinting after him, certain they hadn't even bothered pursuing him beyond the car park – but still… you never know. That doubt, coupled with his reluctance to look over his shoulder, drove him on.

Dad made that supermarket sound like some kind of leisure centre, where you could go, like a day out. What a load of rubbish. If Dad banged on about Marsdens again, Kevan would – well, he'd do nothing because he wasn't supposed to be there.

Dad worked near here, on a big industrial estate further back from the Supermarket. Kevan gave the estate a wide berth, but he didn't double-back on himself. He was going south, getting further and further away from Kevan #1, away from the part of town he knew. But he had no plan, so he just kept pedalling.

There was a square bordered in places by bricks climbing no more than ankle high, with rubble here and there, and beyond that, a playground. Then the fronts of the first row of terraces, grey stone and grey slate, and both windows – one below, one above – hidden by a sodden yellow rectangle of chipboard, the door a gunmetal grey grille. Old smashed by new, Victorian with a 1980s bodge slapped across it.

Kevan cycled along a back road that connected to the end of each row and stopped. He looked round for the first time for the security guards. The road was empty – no one at the other end.

No one in the houses, either.

Not all the rows were abandoned. There were a few streets much further over, where people still lived, but these rows were empty, and – as the yellow signs with "PRO CONSTRUCTION" and a black-and-yellow symbol said – unsafe. The two rows on the other side had already been demolished. Dad said one or two of the houses there had collapsed after an earthquake on the day Kevan had been born.

Somehow, there were weeds growing out of the bricks and gutters. At some of the drainpipes, even bushes grew. In places roof tiles were missing, exposing rafters that were now slick and rotting. The windows and doors were boarded here too, and all the alleys running down the backs of each terrace were bricked up at either end.

In the distance, Kevan could see part of the old mining site. Some of the sheds were still there but many of the buildings on the far side were long gone. People said a ghost lived there. The headstock and wheel, lower from this position but still prominent, stood at once sad and offensive. He pointed his finger at the top of it, traced an invisible line straight down, through the ground, down... and shuddered. He turned back to the road.

Was Gran's old house on this row? He couldn't even remember what the name of the road was. His cheeks burned. He should know this, should know the whole story. Perhaps they'd told him. Perhaps he'd not listened. It seemed to matter more, now.

He wheeled along the back road, checking the street names. None of them rang a bell. Maybe their road was gone.

Kevan thought he saw someone, turning a corner. He followed without thinking, but there was no-one there. He noticed halfway up a street a front door grille, partly prised open at the top and side of the doorway. It beckoned, but he hesitated.

This whole thing was a complete disaster. He seemed to be bouncing from one bad idea to the next. Anish was better at thinking things through. If he was Anish, what would he do?

Anish would have done his homework on time, so that was a hard question to answer. He never put a foot wrong. He wasn't the brightest in class, and he was a bit too obsessed with sci-fi and fantasy for Kevan's liking, but he had a very ordered mind. He managed to temper some of Kevan's wilder plans. Oh, if only he was here! He'd be able to help.

But maybe he wouldn't. After all, they had fallen out. Maybe they weren't best mates any more.

That was unthinkable. When he saw him next, he would apologise. He'd give anything to have him here – he couldn't think of a single school day since Anish turned up in Four Daniels where they hadn't been together.

Kevan had been frogmarched into the classroom by his Dad, as he had been for the last two weeks of the new school year, but stopped protesting when he saw Miss Daniels speaking with a small boy with black shiny hair.

'Kevan, meet Anish Dessay. Anish, you'll be sat next to Kevan.'

Kevan glided over to him, forgetting to say goodbye to his Dad, who exchanged pleasantries with Miss Daniels.

There was something that drew him to Anish. Perhaps that he was new; perhaps that he didn't look very Welsh; but mainly it was his eyes. He had big, plaintive eyes, and Kevan later learned that he just looked like that and there were often times where he didn't need help.

'Hello.'

'Hello. It's Desai,' Anish murmured.

'What?'

'My surname. It's Desai. Not Dessay.'

That morning, Anish had been sat on a chair while the class surrounded him, asking him to say things, because they sounded so funny. Miss Daniels quickly shooed the class away, but after break she asked Anish questions 'because it's important we all know more about our new classmate.'

'So Anish, where are you from?'

'Bradford.'

'Ah, I see,' she smiled. 'But where are you from originally?'

Anish's eyes darted around. Kevan didn't understand the question either.

'Bradford.'

A couple of classmates tittered. Miss Daniels sighed.

'I mean… your family.'

'Oh. Well, my dad's from India.'

'That's what I meant.'

'But my ma's from Brad–'

'So you're originally from India,' Miss Daniels had said, enthusiastic and interested.

During first break of that day, Kevan had found him skulking behind the steps near the "Girls" door, playing with Micro Machines. He explained that he was just looking for a quiet place. Since then it had been their spot.

Well, Kevan thought as he looked around at the dereliction, an abandoned house was as quiet a place as you could get. Anish would approve. Kevan pushed the grille further out and wrestled his BMX through the gap in the side and into the hallway.

The stripped floorboards were instead carpeted in bird poo and feathers, leaves and crumbled plaster. He leaned his BMX against the wall and stepped further in.

A door to the right, leading to a room; another room dead ahead; at a right angle, a set of stairs leading up between them. Graffiti everywhere. Most of it was initials, but some of the more detailed efforts were from two people who clearly didn't like each other. There was the occasional cartoon willy.

The back room had an old stove, with panels missing. No flue. Next to it, a coal scuttle. He looked in – no coal, but in a low wicker basket to the side, wads of flattened newspaper and a few damp matches.

He picked up the newspaper. The top page was badly yellowed but still legible – *Montgomeryshire Express and Radnor Times, Tuesday, October 26, 1965*. The papers were reluctant to separate, but when they did, he could see there were about six or seven editions, going back in time week on week. So the top one was perhaps one of the last papers to be delivered to the house.

He walked into a small extension where a kitchen unit stood. All the other appliances had been taken. There was a door to the backyard. He tried the handle and the door eventually gave. The backyard was a small square, where a clothesline still hung and a coal bunker stood, now empty.

He put the papers on the bunker and peered over the back gate.

The alley was probably cobbles but the grass was so tall he couldn't be sure. At each end of the alley ivy climbed over the bricked-up barriers. A fox stood, motionless, eyeing Kevan.

Mam said she and Gran were evicted a few days after the funeral. That bit of the story Kevan did remember; how someone could be so cruel, knowing what had happened. They stayed with Jackie and her parents for nearly a year until Gran got enough money together to rent another terrace. He wondered if he'd even have lived in Valley Hill if that family hadn't been so kind. Actually, Mam would probably never have met Dad so he wouldn't have even been born.

Kevan picked up the papers and moved back inside. There were no obvious stains or smells in the alcove next to the stove, so Kevan sat down there, and slowly unzipped his rucksack. He yawned; a long, jaw-aching yawn, and he slurped back saliva. He'd been awake – how long? He looked at his watch. That just told him he was a day ahead. He'd fallen asleep in the pantry… must have been about two in the morning… and then Mam came down about seven. Five hours sleep. That wasn't too bad; he should be able to carry on until his mission was complete.

He took out the textbook and the pad. The pad was a bit tatty and damp on the back and edges, probably from the adventure playground. Probably from anywhere he'd been this morning. He placed the old newspapers on top of his rucksack.

He yawned again. He looked at the textbook page about anthracite. Anthra-bloody-cite. Maybe this was what jet-lag felt like?

*Come on, Bevan, get on with it.*

A door slammed shut somewhere – probably in a neighbouring house, he thought, dreamily. Little Owen said that squatters lived in these houses. Perhaps that was the door slamming. Looking at the bird poo and damp in *this* house, he doubted that there was anyone–

81

Floorboards creaked above. Kevan needed no more encouragement. He got to his feet, packed his stuff, got his BMX and pushed out of the front door.

The rain had eased but the wind blew down the street. It felt like a wild west town or something.

He wasn't going to get any work done here, regardless of the shelter some of these houses afforded. He wasn't keen on the next tactic but it might provide options that he hadn't considered yet, so it was worth the risk. It wasn't a quiet place, but he'd tried that.

It was time to go to town.

# Chapter 12

Kevan cycled through the pedestrian arch of the gate, onto the high street. Even with the pouring rain, shoppers gave him a double-take, or the side-eye. Some even tutted (although that might have been his BMX skills).

This wasn't a time-travel caper. It was like someone forced him to bunk off school, and if he got caught, the Universe would be annihilated. There wasn't anything fun about that. Marty McFly defeated bullies with his skateboard and all the girls fancied him. Kevan got to wheel his crappy BMX in the drizzle, looking for shelter.

Wherever he went that had chairs, he'd be scowled at, harried, blocked, questioned. The tearooms, the hairdressers, the bookies; even when Kevan sat in the *Star Wars* arcade machine in the Amusements, the cashier dude – who happily changed his pocket money into ten tens most Saturdays – simply thumbed to the door and said 'Out'.

The high street seemed to be shut down to him. All the doors were open, but his uniform created an invisible barrier. He zipped his coat up to hide his shirt and tie, but too late – PC Richards frowned at him, so Kevan swerved past a bollard and turned down an alley.

Along the town wall and between the buildings that backed onto it were alleys galore. Kevan had explored every single one of them for as long as he could remember. In fact, he knew more or less every street in Bumptown – what each contained, where each came out. And these alleys, their ancient turns and hidden entrances, were a part of that world. He cycled, swerved, skidded. PC Richards was nowhere to be seen.

He came out near the boring bit of the high street – some kind of town hall or council building, the tiny hospital, and across, a building that made him look twice.

The library.

He'd only been there once, during Mam's first and final attempt to get him borrowing books. It had tables, chairs, and what's more, people were *encouraged* to sit and read. It was perfect.

Kevan left his BMX outside, marched through the double doors, and strode up to the counter. Wangle time.

The man at the counter was gangly and hairy, and with each question his head would start tilted up, and lower slowly, like he was watching a spider descending a thread.

'So... you're from Valley Hill Primary?'

'Yep.'

'And... you're doing a project?'

'Uh-huh.'

'Which is why... you want to use the... facilities?'

'Yes.'

'But... you'll only be here for an hour before you go back to school?'

Kevan hadn't said anything of the sort. Still, he found himself nodding in sync.

'Okay.'

He remembered the smell – dust and damp at the same time, with a mix of leather and disinfectant. The walls were shiny, light yellow at the top half with a red brick divider and dirty green at the bottom half.

The old section had rows of dark wooden bookcases up to the ceiling, and a couple of tiny desks against the wall.

There were two people at the bookshelves; a small woman in a green cardigan and stiff skirt and a man in a teal and magenta shell suit, a tracksuit made of crinkly, puffy and highly flammable material. The newer section was metal frame shelving and there were tables arranged in fours to make a large square. More importantly, there was no one in that section. Kevan sat down, opened his bag and brought out his gear, noting that he'd unwittingly taken the newspapers from the abandoned terrace.

Whereas last time he found the place perhaps the most boring building he'd ever been dragged to, this time he felt like it was some kind of safe space. The silence was welcome, invigorating even. With a slight thrill, he arranged his clipboard, textbook and pen neatly and squarely, rested his wrists against the edge of the table, took a breath and began.

He was halfway down the page when an old woman in a cardigan and cat-eye glasses on a chain slowed as she passed him. He covered his work as if she was going to copy off him.

Although he would never admit this to Mr Carter, he had started to find the subject a little bit interesting. Bumptown coal burned longer, hotter and cleaner than the best Anthracite found anywhere in the world. The seam existed on Valley Hill but in none of the surrounding valley slopes. It was a mystery why this was the case.

Well... maybe he could find out here? There was a "Local" section with loads of books, the titles of which were a variation on the "History of Valley Hill" theme.

No – concentrate. He had to get this done. And also, anything that wasn't in the textbook would arouse suspicion. He would be accused of using Anish, or cheating in some other way.

Kevan wandered over to the old section anyway.

The woman was sat at the small desk; Shellsuit was still at the wooden bookcases.

He found a large book on *A History of Valley Hill,* and one on *Valley Hill Colliery* itself. He carried them back to his table.

He flicked through the book on Valley Hill; considering there was only one farm on the whole area, that section had almost as many pages devoted to it as the castle. There were photos of cattle, rosettes, trophies. He flicked again, past "Wales In Bloom" awards, past pictures of geologists in hard hats and diagrams of different theories as to how the hill was formed, until he got to the mining bit.

It was weird; the section concentrated on the coal and how fancy it was, but the bit on the disaster was really short. It was about four paragraphs, and one small photo.

He opened the other book. There was a lot of dense text, but there was a thin glossy bit in the middle so he flicked to that.

There was a photo of the mine from the early 1900s. Another of a man in a suit stood outside the mine-owner's house, which Mr Protheroe now lived in. There was one of blackened men glaring at the camera as they streamed through high gates. That was about 1930. There was another photo of about seven miners stood in a line, laughing: 1952. Then a photo of men stood around a brazier, another of men lining the road to the main gates, some with signs. Another with a man, woman and two children in a room like the one he'd been in just an hour ago. All of those were 1962. And then a photo of stretcher bearers near the headstock. He read the inscription: 'Hours after the explosion which killed 92 miners, April 16th, 1965.'

Then the fire alarm sounded and his heart thumped. He gaped at his pad – only halfway. Shellsuit and the small lady exited; Kevan packed and shouldered his rucksack before he scuttled out.

Back in the rain.

He pressed against the stone wall between two high windows to get some shelter. Hopefully it would be a false alarm and he could get back in there. Gangly stood on the other side of the front door, remonstrating with Cat-eyes. They glanced at him twice; perhaps it was time to leave again. He turned to get his BMX.

But it was gone. He did that thing when you panic and re-imagine the past. He knew he'd propped it under the second window to the right of the door. But he looked around the outside of the whole building for it, in case he'd actually put it elsewhere. Which, of course, he hadn't.

He came back to the entrance, looking again, hoping that somehow the BMX was now there. He was about to promise himself he would come back and replace it, so that it would now reappear somewhere, but he forgot three things:

1. It didn't work last time;

2. He didn't know where his BMX was; and

3. He was never going to travel again.

His heart leapt once more – PC Richards was marching down the hill to him. Kevan turned and ran.

But this time, PC Richards ran too.

# Chapter 13

Kevan breathed hard. He had run for so long that his gums were aching. He had options but none gave him any particular advantage. He could go in the old Arcade below the town clock, which had small stalls and tight corners. He could try the alleys again. Or he could go through the New Arcade. He chose the latter, not for what it offered inside, but for what was out the back of it.

The New Arcade was actually 20-odd years old, but it was newer than the other one, so the name stuck. He pushed through the doors and along the main walkway, his steps clattering over the speckled white mezzanine. Richards wasn't far behind. Gwen was nowhere to be seen, of course. It was lunchtime; she could have been sat outside the Rumblin' Tum, sipping on a milkshake, and he could have run past. A bit like Marty McFly in 1955. Typical.

He burst out of the back door, into the car park, where he found a chance to get some distance from PC Richards.

On Thursdays the car park was fenced off for the cattle market, and on that day it was always busy – although there was only one farm on Valley Hill itself, farmers across the whole valley brought livestock here – but now it was empty, save the fences. There were walkways, pens, platforms – but it just looked like a tangle of vertical posts and horizontal poles if you were running and weren't familiar with the layout. Kevan was; his Gran took him all the time when he was young.

He didn't remember much about it. It was pretty boring. The announcer would chatter – in Welsh, or English, he initially struggled to tell because he spoke so fast – over the appearance of each animal. But then there would be the murmurs whenever the Bumptown farm owner brought out his cattle. Kevan could never tell the difference between them and the out-of-towners' cattle, and the Ridgeway farmers didn't help. With each cow or lamb brought out they would say the same thing. 'So big,' 'So strong,' 'Just look at the posture,' etc etc.

Even though it was Friday, the fences were still up; Kevan ran around the walkways, hairpinning, crossing, until he saw PC Richards exit the Arcade backdoor. There was a central walkway but it didn't take you to the car park exit. Kevan was just able to slip through the gaps between the fencing poles, whereas Richards had to keep hairpinning because of his bulk. Kevan got closer and closer to the exit this way, but any gains for him were lost when he cracked his head ducking under the final fence. He had to run up onto a platform and jump over a perimeter fence to regain some distance.

He ran, past the toilet block and attendant's hut, under the gate and back onto the main Westgate road. He doubled back, hoping to re-enter the high street from the main archway before Richards saw. He bolted through the archway, not daring to check.

The bunting no longer flickered by overhead – now it loomed slowly. His calves and hamstrings ached and twitched. He'd never run this much in all his life. His eyes were becoming sore from the sweat dripping into them. The clouds above looked stormy, moving and swirling, but the rain had stopped briefly and he was heating up something terrible in his coat.

He glanced back – Richards shifting through the archway. No chance for a rest either.

And just at his sweatiest, most ragged moment, there, sat on the wall near the Cenotaph at the fork in the road, her trainers shining through a gaggle of high school students, was Gwen Roberts and her gang.

He didn't have his BMX, so no wheelies. How was he going to impress her?

His exhausted mind rattled through films that might inspire him to be cool, and he came up short. No skateboard, like Marty McFly. No gadgets, like Data in *The Goonies*. No props at all. He couldn't skate anyway but that was beside the point. He had to just act cool in some way.

And then it came to him: *Ferris Bueller's Day Off.*

He'd not seen the whole film but he'd seen a few bits on Film 87 with Barry Norman when it was repeated on Sunday mornings. And more importantly, he'd caught the end by sneakily rewinding the last few minutes of Dad's rental before he returned it to the video shop.

Ferris Bueller is quick, smart, and lucky. He's pulled a sickie; his parents believe he's genuinely ill and they've left him in bed. Instead, he goes out to have fun with his friends. His sister knows his schemes and while driving their mam home, she sees Ferris on his way back even though he's supposed to be laid up; cue a race, Ferris on foot, desperate to get back home and in bed, his sister in the car, determined to get home first and catch him out. Ferris is garden-hopping, taking short cuts. And then he runs past two women sunbathing. He stops, comes back, introduces himself, shakes hands. At his most desperate, with the fate of his entire day – and the trust of his parents – in the balance, Ferris Bueller still takes the time to stop and chat someone up.

That was it.

He would run past the group and then double-back, introduce himself, say goodbye, run off, then Richards would run past in pursuit. A 'Who was that kid?' kind of thing. And Gwen would hopefully wonder.

He had to cross the road to approach them, which made him seem a little less spontaneous, but he had just enough energy to do it. And even if he was caught – preferably out of sight – at least he would have got Gwen's attention.

It was girls and boys from Gwen's year, but there were older boys too. One was called Darren, he was spotty, and he had been blamed for setting fire to one of the new builds at the bottom of the Old West Road. But they didn't scare him, especially now, now that he had a plan to win Gwen's heart.

They were talking and laughing, shrieking and shouting. They were playing music on a ghetto blaster. It was guitar music but nothing he'd heard – not Bon Jovi, not Europe; definitely not Transvision Vamp. He hadn't heard it on his most recent *Now* tape. Maybe it was that "baggy" music that Jamie Williams talked about all the time. He was the coolest kid in Valley Hill Primary so he would know.

He ran past. They didn't notice. He stopped and doubled back. Richards was closer than he'd calculated.

'Hey,' Kevan gasped, in the American way. They still didn't notice. His gums ached so bad. The sweat was cooling quickly. Richards was near the Freeman Hardy Willis, about to cross the road.

'Hey,' he said, louder. They carried on laughing and chatting amongst themselves. One glanced at him, but nothing more.

'Oi!' he yelled, almost a scream. The group stopped and looked at him, alarmed. The music blared into the silence. He had their attention now.

And then Kevan Bevan puked. Bright yellow torrents of it. And worse still, he tried to stop it. He slapped his hand against his mouth and it increased the pressure, so that it exploded out, all of the scrambled egg, all the water, out to the sides, through his fringe, through his fingers in squirting streams of chunder. The crowd leapt back, repelled. Someone screamed. Then Kevan took his hand away to try to say something and there was another long gush. It spattered over his shoes. He looked up, his eyes, nose and mouth streaming with tears, snot and vomit. Gwen had flecks of it on her trainers, on her legs, even her skirt.

'I'm Kevan–'

He spat stringy bile and it swung down onto his trousers. He wiped it against himself and looked up, his eyes watering still.

'Kevan Bevan,' he groaned, not even really at Gwen, and then turned to run before Richards had him.

No one was wondering who he was now.

He'd made sure of that.

# Chapter 14

Kevan's stomach ached more than his legs now; he was cramping in both but his midriff was winning the battle.

He had to think differently about how he was going to get away from PC Richards. The guy was big, but Kevan was also unfit. His legs were springy and wobbly – running was no longer an option.

But the alleys were.

They were some of the oldest bit of the walled town, apart from the castle at the top. They looped, doubled back, in some cases just stopped at a dead end. They were Kevan's escape route.

He ducked and skittered, dodged and weaved over the cobbles and stones. But this time his steps were a billion times noisier and sounded out ahead and behind, almost like they were happening before and after him, until his steps were indistinguishable from PC Richards's. Maybe the alleys weren't such a good idea after all. He got dizzy; the sharp turns made the corners come at him from the sides.

He found a narrow gap between a jeweller and a tobacconist where he squeezed in and held his breath. The clattering footsteps continued, loud and not changing in volume, so Kevan had no idea where Richards was until the last moment, when his heavy steps became clear and sharp, and he puffed past.

The walls were so tight against Kevan's chest that he had to breathe out, but slowly. He peered out; Richards slowed as he came near to the entrance back onto the high street, and leant a hand on a cast iron bollard. He looked both ways, then turned. Kevan got his head back in.

Richards clumped slowly around. He stopped, his words broken up by ragged breaths.

'Boy, h-if you come out now, I'll take you back to school and no questions asked. Jesus. But if you don't, h-I'll... I'll make a report, h-and visit your school, and you'll... you'll be in a lot of trouble. Oh, oh god. Come on, boy – make the right choice.'

He said "Boy" twice. He hadn't heard Kevan identify himself to Gwen and her gang. PC Richards didn't know who he was. And his rising frustration confirmed it.

'This isn't, isn't Welshpool – there are rules.'

Kevan didn't move a muscle.

Richards huffed and then stomped off. Kevan waited for five full minutes, getting his breath back.

He looked past bollards to the narrow view of the high street. Shoppers, passing back and forth, on the near pavement, on the far one.

And then Mam.

It couldn't be. She hadn't been on the high street for as long as Kevan could remember. And the figure was in view for a mere second. And stepping back out onto the high street on the off-chance it was Mam would be madness, given Kevan's pursuer was still on the prowl.

Kevan stepped out and crept to the building edge, just past the bollard, and looked around the corner.

The figure certainly looked like Mam. Same coat, same build. She seemed folded in on herself, but that might just be the horrible weather.

Kevan followed, scanning for PC Richards as he went.

94

The woman crossed; if anyone else recognised her – and it was such a small town most would – they didn't show it.

She walked up, past the library, on the side of the castle where the Memorial Gardens were.

Some fancy-pants businessman had donated a load of money for the Memorial Gardens to be built, for the 20th Anniversary of the disaster. Mam had never been. Kevan had, but only to bounce the conifers near the back (a process involving taking a running jump and holding on for dear life). From the outside it was tall evergreens and a path around the outside of it which gave bracing views of...well, the rooves of the high street. Perhaps the farmland beyond.

The woman stopped near the steps to the entrance.

Kevan hid near an information board by the castle ruins.

The woman didn't move. Finally, she glanced down, turned and walked off.

Kevan wasn't sure any more that this was Mam. She didn't walk in the same way. This woman's steps were uneven, like she was a bit drunk. And Mam hardly ever drank.

Kevan shook his head out of the reverie. He scanned once more for PC Richards.

He had a plan. It was suicidal, but it had been that kind of day.

Time for school.

*

Kevan came through the town wall and edged across the pebbley ground between the Community Hall and Conservative Club. Across the road, in front of the Methodist Church, the Jesus/Ian Rush joke beckoned. He looked both ways – for PC Richards and for traffic – and dashed over.

He crouched by Ian Rush. He felt like he felt whenever it rained on a school day: BMX-less. Which, roughly translated, meant slow and ploddy.

He hadn't really had a plan in any case of how to get finished homework to Kevan #1 if #1 was in school – it would probably have involved hanging around outside, at the railings down by the "Girls" door, until #1 and Anish came out at lunch. But now, he had unfinished homework, he'd run out of ideas for shelter, and he'd nearly run out of time. He had to get completed homework to #1 before his confrontation with Ya-Ya; it made some kind of crazy sense to finish the homework at his final destination. He was somehow going to get into school and find somewhere secluded inside.

12:53: lunch was in seven minutes. Could he just open the gate and march through the main entrance? The saplings and climbing frame did provide cover, so maybe he could sneak up on the infants' side so that #1 didn't see him. Or he could wait for the lunch delivery from the high school, climb into the big food cart, and sneak out before it got to the main hall.

No – that only worked in *Flight of the Navigator*. This was real life. He'd just have to go with the more straightforward option.

But where would he go, once he was in? There were classrooms either side which he had to steer clear of, not to mention the Head-Teacher's office, the Caretaker's room and the staff lounge.

No, the best bet would be to sneak into the main toilets, and just hope that he didn't bump into anyone.

Was there a padlock on the gate? He put a hand against it and pushed. It gave easily, so he stepped forward.

A hand gripped his shoulder. It pinched.

'Gotcha.'

Kevan didn't even need to turn. He just knew. Bumptown was so pokey that there was almost no point running. Everyone collided into each other two minutes later anyway. If he had his BMX...

PC Richards shook his head, but still managed to look smug, even with the sweat matting his sideburns.

'I gave you a chance, boy.'

This man was going to march him into school and report him to Mrs Peters. She was going to tell him off, then march him back to class. Then the class was going to see him and Kevan #1 in the same room. Then the world was going to explode, and the Universe was going to disintegrate. Everyone was going to die.

'You don't understand,' Kevan said.

'Try me.'

Kevan looked at him, sized him up, shook his head.

'Nah.'

Richards's grip tightened, his thumb digging into Kevan's collarbone.

'Ow!'

'Come on. Let's hear your excuses.'

Maybe he should run again? There was a lot at stake. Richards wouldn't even understand in the future if he kept it a secret, but at least Kevan would know the truth.

He slowly moved his arm forward. He was going to elbow Richards in the ribs, then swing his forearm up and back and smash his fist into his face, like Bruce Lee. It was the only way.

But then Richards's grip loosened.

'What's going on here?'

Kevan looked at the gate. Mr Protheroe stood on the other side of it.

'Oh,' Richards said. 'Good morning, Mr Protheroe. I've just caught this boy playing truant.'

Mr Protheroe opened the gate and stood on the step. 'Well, that can't be right. I'm not quite sure what this young man was doing out in the playground–'

'He's on the pavement, Mr Protheroe. That's–'

'–but he's been in class all day.'

PC Richards shifted his weight onto the other foot.

'I've just chased him across town.'

'Not possible, Constable. He's been in the same room as me for the last hour or so. And if I bring his teacher out, he'll say the same thing.'

'Well, I'll take him in and we can straighten it out one way or the other,' Richards said, gathering himself to full height.

'I tell you what,' Mr Protheroe said, clapping his hand on PC Richards' shoulder in turn, 'You leave him with me and I'll make sure he gets back to his class. If it turns out that I'm going doolally and he hasn't in fact been in class this morning, then I'll be in touch with your superiors to ensure that you're commended for your dogged perseverance.'

'That's not how–'

'Have you written this incident down in your book?'

'No – but–'

'Then according to your records this didn't even happen.'

'I haven't had time–'

'Is your boss CI Fields?'

'Er… yes.'

'Ah, yes. Derek. We go back years. I'm sure if I were to tell Derek how well you're doing, he'll make sure you're justly recognised.'

It sounded like Mr Protheroe was being kind to PC Richards, but the officer looked angry and frustrated. Kevan didn't care, as long as he went along with it. And sure enough, he took his hand off Kevan's shoulder and stepped back.

Kevan turned. PC Richards did the eye-finger gesture – *I'll be watching you.*

Mr Protheroe smiled at Richards as he backed away, then shone the same smile onto Kevan.

'Let's get you back in, eh? Can't have you running around on your own.'

They both walked across the playground, along the saplings. Kevan looked back – PC Richards glared through the railings. Kevan gave him a "Hacksaw" thumbs-up.

'So, you're reading your homework first, is that right?'

If I can get half an hour of peace and quiet, Kevan thought, as he nodded politely.

'And what is yours about?'

'Coal. Different types.'

'Ah, yes – the famous Valley Hill Coal.'

They reached the main door.

'Your… grandfather worked there, didn't he?'

'Yeah. He died in the explosion.'

'Yes,' Mr Protheroe said softly, opening the door. 'I suppose that's too painful to write about.'

'No,' Kevan shrugged. 'I never knew him. Mr Carter didn't want me to write about it, though.'

'Oh. Well, maybe one day you can tell me all about it.'

'Okay.'

They walked into the entrance hall, the infants' library to their left. This wasn't any better – whether it was Richards, Protheroe, Peters or Carter, the Universe was still in danger of exploding if he walked into that classroom.

'You look like you could do with a quick freshen up, young man. Why don't you pop to the toilets before lunch starts?'

*Jackpot.*

'Yes, sir.'

'Good lad.' Mr Protheroe walked toward the hall and began talking with a dinner lady.

Kevan entered the toilets and looked at his crumpled face in the mirror. Red, blotchy, sweaty and clammy from the rain, his eyes still managed to glint at his stroke of luck. Mind you, he was due a break.

He washed his hands and face. He was already wet from the rain, so he just pulled some paper towels and pressed them against himself. He then hid in the toilet cubicle, took out his clipboard and textbook, and carried on writing.

# Chapter 15

Through the crack in the toilet door, Kevan could see Kevan #1 and Anish finishing up their lunch. He opened it wider with his left hand while his right hand clutched his completed homework. He had to get it to Anish, and he had to time it just right.

His plan was to hide near the "Girls" door until #1 blagged his way past Mrs Wells into the main entrance. Then he would open the "Girls" door to the outside steps, find Anish, pretend to be #1, and give him the homework, using some flimsy pretence. It didn't matter what – as long as there was no overlap of Kevans it would be fine. #1 would wonder where the homework – in his handwriting – came from, but he would readily accept it to get out of trouble.

Kevan closed the door as #1 and Anish clattered toward the main entrance, and opened it again.

Once #1 went into the classroom for the textbook, Kevan couldn't use the main entrance to get to Anish because of Mrs Wells stationed out front, and of course he didn't want anyone seeing two Kevan Bevans at once and going blind, or their face melting, or whatever. Which meant that if he was to monitor the order of events, he had to get across the hall and to the "Girls" corridor right now.

So he did what he did best – wangled with confidence.

He marched across the hall, head held high – even had the time to wink and do finger guns at an infant – then got past the coats and into the darkness near the "Girls" door.

Next to his classroom were two large square ceramic sinks. He climbed onto one and opened the small window, giving himself a restricted view of the playground. Anish and #1 moved past, disappearing round the corner toward the steps. He climbed down, counted 60 seconds – for #1 to realise he had no textbook – and then walked quickly back across the hall to the main entrance.

There was #1, blocked by Mrs Wells.

Kevan moved on, past Mrs Peters' office, and peered out of another small window onto the Infants' side. There was a young boy, inspecting an ant – but where was the pile-on? At this rate #1 was going to get marched in by the dinner lady and his cover blown.

There was nothing for it – Kevan stuck his head out the window.

'Pile-on!' he shouted.

The ant inspector suddenly found himself the starting point; two children dutifully leapt onto him. Within seconds six infants squirmed in a confused pile, and Miss Wells began stomping over to them.

'Hoi!'

Kevan looked back into the main entrance hall; Kevan #1 skimmed past the Infants Library and across the Dinner Hall. Kevan followed at a distance and again marched across the hall, just after #1 snuck into the classroom. If anyone saw them, they'd just think it was déjà vu.

He opened the heavy "Girls" door, flinching at a non-existent alarm. Then down the steps. Anish was there, waiting.

'Dezzy,' Kevan said, almost tearful that he finally had a friendly face to talk to.

'That was quick. What happened? You look – you smell–'

'Yeah I know. No time.' Kevan pulled his homework out of his rucksack.

'I got it done. It's all here. But I need you to keep hold of it and give it back to me when I come back out to the playground.'

'Why? Where are you going?'

'Just got to tie up some loose ends. Oh, and Dezzy? Go and hang around near the trees. I'll see you straight away. And stay away from Ya-Ya.'

'Er... Okay.'

'Great. Thanks bud,' Kevan said, clapping him a little too hard on the arm.

Anish's eyes flicked to the ground.

'Er...Kev–'

'No time, Dezzy.'

Kevan slipped back in through the "Girls" door and crept to his classroom door.

Mr Carter was eating his Chicken Supreme. The store cupboard door was open a crack; #1 would be peering out. Where was that kid who interrupted him? If he didn't turn up, #1 would be trapped all lunch. And he needed him out of there to retrieve his homework.

He waited, checked the clock – 13:35. His presence had somehow had a knock-on effect and altered things. Infants not doing pile-ons. Anish moved from the steps. And now that kid not turning up. This time-travel lark was simply too much to follow. There was no way of not making some kind of mess of the smallest incident.

Before he could gather his wits he knocked on the door and opened it.

'Come in, why don't you?' Mr Carter said.

If he could re-enact what the other kid did… it didn't need to be spot on, just something to get Mr Carter to the board…and his back turned… and perhaps if the kid did turn up, he would see Mr Carter was busy and not bother.

Mr Carter looked him up and down, and turned his chair to face him.

'What happened to you? How can you get covered in mud so quickly? And where did the mud even come from?'

Kevan was certain of one way to get Mr Carter to the blackboard; he just had to steal the other boy's idea. He hadn't heard clearly what the boy had said, but based on Mr Carter's response, it was something to do with pronouncing words.

'Please sir, I've been going over my homework for the presentation thing and I can't say some of the words.'

'Ah I see. Yes, fair enough – you lot didn't know you were reading it out, I suppose. Let me get a textbook.'

It was weird hearing him say exactly the same thing again. It was like he was reading from a script.

Mr Carter opened his desk drawer. Kevan looked over at the cupboard, the key sticking out, gleaming. Mr Carter moved some papers on his desk. Kevan quickly produced his own textbook from his rucksack.

'Ah, you've got one there. Okay, let's see then.'

'It's just these words sir,' Kevan mumbled, pointing vaguely at the coal types, as he saw the cupboard door open over Mr Carter's shoulder. Mr Carter put the textbook down and wrote each term on the blackboard, before pointing at the first.

'So this is "Anthracite". "An-Thra-Cite".'

Kevan's face went cold as he saw #1's hand reach for the textbook. He stiffened up.

'My goodness, boy, are you okay? Have you been ill?'

'I'm fine, sir.'

'Hmmm. Let's leave this for now – in fact, I'll say this to the class so that everyone knows, so thank you for pointing it out to me. In the meantime, you need to go see Miss Simmons so she can look you over.'

Kevan glanced at the door to the canteen. #1 had gone.

'Okay sir,' Kevan said, and backed away to the side-door.

He wasn't going to see the nurse yet. The mission wasn't over.

He snuck back to the sinks and looked out of the window. #1 passed by below him, toward the steps. There was Anish further back, near the saplings – but Ya-Ya and Hughesy were crowding him, so he was hard to see. #1 passed by again, scanning the playground as he made his way back to the entrance. Kevan couldn't yell out.

He caught a glance of Anish's face. Bemused, hangdog. Like when Ya-Ya called him "Chips and Rice". But this time Kevan couldn't protect him. He felt a rage fizz inside.

Shortly, Ya-Ya and Hughesy moved away, falling out of sight as they headed in the direction of the main entrance. They had unwittingly kept Anish from Kevan #1, kept him from getting that homework to his best friend, kept him from preventing what was to come next.

Kevan edged toward the corridor, his stomach churning at the inevitable. Kevan #1 was now sat in the canteen, head down, trying to do his homework. And then he could see two dark figures loping down the corridor across the hall. Hughesy ducked into the toilets and Ya-Ya came into the canteen and sat across from #1. Then #1 stood up. Then Ya-Ya harried him. Then #1 pushed Ya-Ya and called him – called him that name. Then he heard Mr Carter's voice bark from the far canteen door of the classroom. Then they both sloped into the classroom.

Kevan looked back out of the window – Anish, stood alone, his shoulders drooped, as he turned and slowly began to walk in the direction of the "Girls" door steps. Kevan climbed down from the sink and peered into the classroom from the side-door. Two red-faced boys and one red-faced teacher.

He heard the "Girls" door creak open. Was it Anish? #1 would be coming out soon, so Kevan stood among the coats.

Anish closed the door behind him. He looked like he'd been crying. He still had Kevan's homework in his hand, as well as #1's rucksack, now wet. This was an odd situation. If Anish got the homework to Kevan #1 before #1 confessed to not doing any homework, there was still a slim hope. He'd had Action Slips before, for swearing, shoving and lying; even though he was currently getting told off for the first two, it wasn't Mr Carter's "Triple Whammy" yet. And the homework was good. Perhaps the best he'd ever–

Ya-Ya stormed out of the side-door and wiped his nose on his sleeve. His head snapped round at Anish. He marched over and whipped the A4 sheet out of his hands.

'What's this?'

'Homework.'

'Yours?'

Ya-Ya glanced at the rucksack in Anish's other hand, and before Anish could even respond, Ya-Ya tore the homework into shreds and dropped it to the ground. He then jerked toward Anish, who flinched. Ya-Ya smiled – a hateful smile, a sneer, a grin, a glare all at once – and stomped off.

Kevan's best mate crouched and slowly gathered the shreds from the parquet as Kevan himself – original Kevan, not Kevan #1 – sobbed silently behind a pile of coats.

# Chapter 16

After the bell, more kids piled coats onto Kevan as he stood below the hooks, dejected, struggling to breathe.

The plan was shot. Nothing Kevan had done had changed anything. They were right back where they started. Next on the list – Action Slip. Then lines. Then falling out with Anish.

Anish.

His best mate had been there all along, waiting for him. He'd even come through the "Girls" door, which was possibly the naughtiest thing Anish Desai had ever done. And for the rest of the day Kevan #1 was going to glare at him, and then start an argument with him on the way home. No wonder Anish looked so upset when he stomped off into his house.

Kevan remembered that #1 went to the toilet just before they started reading their homework – he considered confronting him, telling him to stay there until home-time, and he would march into Mr Carter's classroom and recite his homework with no paper at all. That would dazzle them.

But even though he found the subject interesting, and even though he'd read, re-read, and written and re-written about coal, Kevan could barely remember any of it. Now he was cold, wet, tired, hungry, and covered in blood, sweat and tears. And puke. If he stood in front of the class to present, he would probably faint. Not to mention that he was scared of what would happen if he did confront himself.

Would #1's memory of that encounter appear in his own head?

He saw #1 cross the hall to the far corridor, and let him go.

Kevan slipped out of the "Girls" door as the rain started to fall once more, and crept around the front of the school, under the high windows, and skirted the saplings to the front gate. He let himself out and walked toward the Methodist Church. He stood for a moment, gathering himself. It was too early to go home – if Mam saw him in the porch she'd want to know why he was there. He gazed absently at the Parish notices – coffee mornings, Lego club, a service on the 16th April – Easter Monday – at the Memorial Gardens, to mark 25 years... the coffee morning was over, being the afternoon and all, and the Lego club wasn't on til seven o'clock. And he'd been to Lego club before and the Lego was battered and you could only really make blocks of things. His cousins had Technics Lego, which had really cool parts to it. This was not that.

He glanced back at the sign. That was one place he hadn't thought of, even though he'd been there earlier – the Memorial Gardens. There were sheltered benches in there. If he re-wrote his homework, he could give it to Anish at afternoon break. It might not change anything, but it was worth one last shot.

He crossed the road and looked over at the school. He saw #1, gazing out of the window at the rain.

And then their eyes met.

At this point Kevan didn't care. Besides, it was raining too hard for #1 to see him clearly. The connection, however weak, seemed to give him strength.

108

'Don't worry Kevan #1 – I won't let you down,' he murmured. 'One way or another we'll get some damn homework handed in.'

And then Mr Protheroe appeared at the window and saw him too. And Kevan stood firm, almost daring the Universe to do something about it.

Earthquake?

Tornado?

Flood?

Nah – just some heavy rain.

And you can only get so wet.

★

The rain had eased by the time he got to the Memorial Gardens. It lay at the top end of the high street, near the castle ruins on the hill, and Kevan was out of breath by the time he passed through the main gates.

Sleeping tulips and perky daffodils, backed by trees whose blossom now burgeoned out of green shoots, lined a central path. Further along, the path forked off to either side of a central sculpture made of cast iron. It was a twisted mass, showing two figures striving up to the sky, while around their legs were shards and split panels. Bordering the flowers here were tall conifers and firs, so that the sculpture seemed to glow against the dark evergreen with light from above. A few steps at the far end led up to a stone monolith with the names of all the victims.

On either side of the monolith were sheltered benches. He sat in one, took out his clipboard and textbook, and started writing. A woman sat on a bench across from him. She was about Mam's age, and beautiful as well, but in a more glamorous way. Her clothes were smart and neat; her hair was immaculate, like the newsreader Anna Ford. She glanced at him and smiled, but she seemed sad at the same time as she looked back down at her magazine.

He thought about Gwen, about the puke spatter on her trainers. He thought about Anish, and the trouble he risked trying to help, of his treatment by that pillock Ya-Ya. This was one last chance; he had to make it worth the tears, the blood. The puke.

The textbook was getting dog-eared even for a hardback; the clipboard was pristine but the paper was curled at the corners and streaked with mud. He started writing and was two paragraphs in before realising he hadn't even looked at the textbook.

Soon he was finished; he unclipped it, and put it against his chest inside his coat, ready to whip it out and stuff it into Anish's hands.

A figure appeared at the gates. From Kevan's position only the helmet was visible.

PC Richards once again.

Kevan slipped out of the shelter and hid behind the monolith.

Richards came to the bottom of the steps.

There was a stand of tall conifers at the back that Kevan and Anish had climbed; he backed toward them. He shimmied up one and tentatively stepped on thin branches until he was round the back of it.

The view was actually quite good from here. You could indeed see the farmland, but also woodland down by the creek. The flashing yellow light of a distant breakdown truck, alongside a lorry. Someone's washing was strewn across a wall, probably from the storm. He pitied those who believed it was over – he certainly wouldn't have climbed this tree an hour ago.

PC Richards entered the sheltered bench and came out with Kevan's rucksack. Was there anything in there to identify him?

'Excuse me,' Richards said to the woman across the way.

She looked up.

'Have you seen the boy whose bag this is?'

'You mean, have I seen the boy to whom this bag belongs?'

'That's what I just asked.'

'It certainly wasn't, Officer.' She closed her magazine. 'But no, I haven't.' She sounded local, but with a strange twang.

PC Richards put his hands on his hips.

'Oh, so this bag just appeared out of nowhere, did it?'

'Possibly. I couldn't say. It's more likely that it was there before I arrived.'

'So, you didn't notice anything?'

'No. But then, I was quite engrossed in this magazine. Did you know they plan to launch a giant telescope into orbit so that it can take pictures of distant galaxies?'

He pulled out some magazines and a few of the old papers. The way he handled them almost made Kevan shout out, but he soon put them back, replaced the rucksack and started looking round the shelter.

And then he disappeared by a conifer at the side.

Kevan knew where he was going to come out – and sure enough, there he was, by the perimeter path. Kevan inched round but branches began to snag and he was stuck momentarily, with PC Richards stood immediately below him. After what felt like an eternity, Richards sloped back into the Gardens.

He started to gather pace, nodded at the woman and went down the steps. Soon he was gone.

Kevan began to step down the branches. His homework slipped out of his coat and blew off, swirling around, ducking behind the monolith.

Kevan took the branches down fast, catching his arms, scratching his hands. He dropped and ran to the monolith. The homework was nowhere to be found.

He looked at the woman sat on the bench. Should he ask her? No – she was reading her magazine. And she was a bit weird. He carried on scrabbling around the monolith. And then he realised that his homework was gone.

'You okay?' she asked. Her voice was gentle.

'Yeah… yeah,' Kevan said, still scanning the ground, the trees, the flowerbeds.

'Okay.' A crackle of magazine.

Kevan stood. What difference would it make? And her voice was enticing; he felt compelled.

'I've lost my homework.'

'Oh.'

'I'm gonna get grounded.'

'Ah.'

'I'm gonna miss Wrestlemania.'

'I see.'

Kevan's shoulders drooped.

'I don't know what to do.'

'Well, by the look of things you've been on a bit of a mission.'

'Yeah.'

'Is there any way to succeed?'

'…I could start all over again…'

'Right.'

Kevan didn't know what else to say. He couldn't time travel all over again. There couldn't be three of him running around. He could hide somewhere else, do the homework somewhere else, but he would still have to go to school with it. He could go home, get grounded, do the homework, go back in time, put it in his rucksack with a note…

'You look like you could do with a hot dinner and bed.'

Kevan burst into tears at the suggestion. It cut through the madness, and heightened his cravings.

The woman's magazine flapped closed.

'Hey, hey, it's okay. I'm sure it's not as bad as you think it is.'

Kevan glared at her. Her eyebrows raised and she put her magazine onto the bench. Her voice went a little hard.

'Is the world ending?'

'No.'

'Have you killed anyone?'

'No.'

Softer: 'Does your Mam and Dad love you?'

More tears. They fell freely.

'Yes.'

'Then go home, sweetheart.'

Kevan wiped his nose with his sleeve and nodded.

He walked past the woman and got to the gate.

'And remember,' she said, 'there's always Summer Slam.'

Kevan turned, unsteady on his feet. She was talking about another wrestling contest in August. He smiled, not looking at anything in particular.

'I never thought of that.' He nodded at her.

The woman smiled back.

★

Kevan sat in the stand of trees past the turning circle in Meifod Crescent, in the pouring rain, waiting for Kevan #1 to slouch down the road. And there he was, wet, slow and downright miserable.

#1 turned and walked down his garden path while thunder rolled; Kevan came out of the trees and walked over the space where the bungalow once stood. #1 was now in the porch, leaning against the inner door. Then he disappeared – no thud or flash. Kevan was about to approach but remembered that he had to wait for #1 to come back, then disappear again. He tried to time it by visualising #1's movements in the past. Go upstairs, see himself, hide in the bathroom, come back down – probably another ten minutes.

He was struggling to keep track of what was going on, but one thing he was certain of – he was in the same position as #1. Just this time he was wetter, tireder, and hungrier.

Kevan's eyes began to close and he leant against the boundary wall. He needed to stay awake because if he missed #1's return he would have to wait extra long just to ensure he didn't encounter him in the porch. Thankfully the lightning and thunder was beginning to synchronise and that was enough to stop him from dozing.

#1 came back, opened the inner door and cheered at Chicken Surprise. A minute later and he disappeared again.

Kevan stood. Time to go home.

A gigantic *crack* and Kevan ducked. Behind him, a rushing, splitting and scorching noise. He turned – one of the trees had been obliterated by lightning, and at least three of the others were on fire, with smoke and steam in equal measure billowing off.

Kevan shrugged.

He shuffled down the path and entered the porch, the shock of the lightning now breaking through his fatigue.

# Chapter 17

The water was so murky Kevan could only see his knees, like shiny pink stones rising from a muddy pond. This was perhaps the first time that he'd enjoyed a bath (although he needed to remind Mam that this one was just Sunday's, done early).

He'd come through the inner door and stood there, shaking from his near miss. Mam had popped her head round the pantry again, and when she saw him, she marched over and fussed over him, the state of him, what was that on his head – was that a cut? Had he fallen off a cliff? Had he been sick? Should she get him to a hospital? It was only while Kevan was in the bath that he realised that from Mam's point of view, her son had come in, celebrated Chicken Surprise, and then when she looked back around, she saw a bedraggled, hopeless wreck. It must have been quite jarring.

Things got weirder when he told them what had happened. Kevan had showed them the Action Slip and blurted out a stream of disasters and confrontations, including time travel, meeting himself, almost blowing up the Universe. He was so tired he couldn't stick to the official report.

It was only when Mam told him to sit down and slow down that he was able to get back on message. He started from the start: that he'd told them that there was no homework when there was, then told Mr Carter he'd done his homework when he hadn't, then tried to rush some, then pushed Ya-Ya and swore at him, then got some lines, then an Action Slip, then fell out with Anish, and this time he stopped talking, even forgetting to mention the lightning strike. He felt like he had been reciting a list of events from long ago; to Mam and Dad some of the things had happened within the last couple of hours.

Mam seemed to take all of this quite well, until he told her the subject of the homework. And even then, he wasn't sure if she was angry – she just murmured that she was going to put the bath on, and disappeared upstairs.

But as Dad shepherded Kevan up the stairs, blue lights started pulsing through the porch, until it and the front room started to look like a very cold disco. Dad called for Mam, and she didn't answer, so they went into Mam and Dad's bedroom and found her there, stood rigid at the window, the blue lights flashing against her. They all looked out.

The rain had stopped and one of the trees was still burning. There was a big blocky fire engine in the turning circle, with firemen stood around watching.

Mam had her arms wrapped around her tightly. She had an queer expression on her face for such a spectacle; she just looked weary.

Kevan dunked his head into the brown water again. When he broke the surface Dad was stood there. He flinched and sprayed water everywhere.

'Sorry pal. You alright?'

He nodded. 'Is Mam still angry with me?'

'No, pal. She wasn't angry with you in the first place.'

He sat on the toilet seat.

'You and Ieaun, eh?'

'He's a div.'

Dad's moustache wiggled. 'Yeah.' He rubbed his hands on his legs, inspected his palms.

'What swearword did you use?'

Kevan blushed. 'Why?'

'Just to make sure. You know… that it's not the bad one.'

'Aren't they all bad?'

'Yeah, but… you know. The worst one.'

Kevan tried to think. He looked at Dad.

'I called him a bloody fluckstake.'

'What's a fluckstake?'

'I don't know.'

Dad stood, turned and started straightening the towel on the radiator. The "B" word surely wasn't the worst one?

'And Mr Carter heard?'

'I shouted it, Dad. Everyone heard.'

Was Dad upset? His shoulders were jerking up and down, and he seemed to be rubbing his eyes.

He turned back.

'Ah, pal.' He was smiling, his face red. Kevan smiled as well, uncertain, but going along with it. He fashioned his hair into a Mohican.

'So Mam wasn't angry with me?'

'Nah.'

'So I'm not grounded?'

'Oh, no, you're definitely grounded pal.'

'Aw.'

'Sorry.'

'But I can have Anish round for Wrestlemania.'

'Ha. Nope.'

'But can I–'

'No, pal. You won't be watching Wrestlemania on your own either.'

Kevan had slipped lower and lower into the bath with each blow. He hadn't asked for any of this. Well, he had forgotten his homework and then explicitly wished to go back in time, but that was beside the point.

He realised that being done was so much better than time travel. Time travel was rubbish. But he wished that Mam had just shouted at him, got angry. Instead, she was quiet, clipped, murmuring.

'Dad, is she okay?'

Dad nodded slowly, with a reassuring squint. When Kevan had first started asking that question a year or so ago, Dad had said 'Who?' Then later it was 'Your mam?' Now, he just knew.

'Yeah, she's fine. Actually, she popped over to Jackie's for a brew this morning, so until you staggered through the door, she'd had a good day.'

Kevan frowned.

'It was a joke, pal.'

'Oh, yeah, I know, hur-hur.'

Dad stood to leave. Kevan's frown immediately resumed.

She hadn't seen Jackie at all. Because Jackie was feeding him scrambled eggs at the supermarket. And, if it was the same woman he'd seen, Mam had just been walking the streets.

Kevan struggled to stop frowning at dinner too. Mam reminded him that it was Chicken Surprise and he forgot to be enthusiastic about it, causing her to shake her head, bemused. This time travel business made it hard to stay consistent.

They ate dinner in silence until the last few minutes. Mam seemed to be cutting her food and moving it around the plate; she did that sometimes. Finally, she put her knife and fork down and rested her arms in along the edge of the table. Her voice was calm, but it was almost worse for it.

'Kevan, did you not think to talk to us about your homework? You know, we could've helped you.'

Kevan shrugged slowly. There wasn't any way to answer this; he never involved them because he couldn't be bothered to do it. And to be frank, they'd never offered to help until now.

'What do we know about coal, Ruth?' Dad said.

Mam looked at him like she'd been slapped.

Dad lowered his head and looked at Kevan.

'You had a textbook for this, didn't you?'

Kevan nodded slowly. Dad nodded back and looked at Mam.

'Why would he treat this homework differently to the others?'

Mam opened her mouth and rearranged her arms into the same position, but didn't answer. Kevan wasn't sure whether Dad was defending him, or criticising him. Dad looked at his plate, glanced at Kevan and smiled weakly. And then Kevan knew.

They argued a bit while he was upstairs. When he was little, he used to tell them both to calm down. Nowadays he would sit at the top of the stairs and listen. Tonight, he stayed in his room and closed the door, and only came down when it had gone quiet.

Later, in the living room, Kevan lay with his head in Mam's lap while *A Song For Europe* was on. Terry Wogan was introducing a teenager called Emma who the whole of Bumptown was rooting for. You wouldn't have known it from Mam and Dad alone; they murmured vague approval regardless of who was singing. Kevan wasn't really listening anyway – he was listening to Mam's tummy, and her heartbeat, lulled by the warmth of her lap.

'Mam?'

'Yeah?'

'Are you both going to get divorced?'

There was a really weird silence.

'No, pal,' Dad said.

'You know, people who love each other very much still have arguments,' Mam said.

'I know.'

'And what me and Dad argue about isn't serious enough to divorce over. It's just sometimes, we... sometimes I... have a tough time of it.'

'Okay,' Kevan said, nestling. 'I just don't want you going to the loony bin.'

Mam laughed. 'The what?'

Kevan gave her the side-eye.

'Ya-Ya's mam and dad split up and she went to the loony bin.'

'I'm not going to the loony bin. And Ya-Ya's mam didn't go to the loony bin.'

'Where did she go, then?'

There was long pause. 'I don't know.'

Kevan gazed at her before settling back.

Emma had finished singing. The audience seemed to like it.

'Mam?'

'Yeah.'

'Why haven't you gone to the Memorial Gardens?'

'Jeez, boy,' Dad muttered, with a rueful smile.

More silence. Kevan was worried she'd shrug him off her lap but she just sat still, breathing slowly.

'I don't need to visit somewhere to... to...'

Kevan turned his head. She looked down and met his eyes.

'I've got my own Memorial.'

She tapped her head.

'In here.'

She patted her chest.

'And in here.'

She smiled kindly. Kevan nestled his head back in position.

Terry Wogan was telling them that the results would be broadcast later that night and that the winner would go on to represent the United Kingdom at *Eurovision* in Zagreb.

'Mam?'

'Yes, Kevan?'

It sounded like this was the last question she would allow. He needed to make it count.

'You know the Chicken Surprise?'

'Mmm?'

'What's the "Surprise"?'

Silence again. Mam's tummy rising and falling slowly.

'It's turkey.'

# Chapter 18

"Will it be chips, or jacket spuds?
Will it be salad or frozen peas?
Will it be mushrooms?
Fried onion rings?
You'll have to wait and see.
Hope it's chips, it chips,
We hope it's chips, it's chips…"

*Birds Eye Steakhouse Advert*
  *to the tune of Que Sera Sera, 1982*

Dad sang this most Saturday mornings when he bustled in from the shops. He always did a terrible Indian accent when he said 'Fried Onion Rings', even though the man who sings it in the advert is clearly from Africa.

'Here we are Ruthie – the best from the high street.'

Mam didn't answer; she'd been quiet since breakfast. The firemen had returned and were busy cutting the damaged trees down. She knew what it meant, knew what it would reveal, which might have been why she hadn't ventured out of the kitchen.

Kevan took a deep breath and tried to plan his day. *Going Live* was on; Phillip Schofield was talking to Su Pollard about something. *The ITV Chart Show* wasn't on for another hour but he was going to miss most of it, because he was going to travel back to yesterday, and he couldn't tape it because he would have to explain why to his parents.

He'd promised himself he wouldn't travel ever again. Forget the Universe, space-time continuums or any other science stuff – travelling was exhausting, demeaning and dangerous. But one of the main things he turned over in his mind, aside from those mind-scrambling time-loops, was his BMX. He needed it back. He'd stood next to Mam at her bedroom window, as she watched the men at work on the trees, and peered into the front garden to see if it had magically appeared; it had not.

Running from PC Richards was difficult enough, but without his BMX he felt even slower. His bike was about to fall apart but it felt almost a part of him. Downhill, no hands, he felt like he was flying. Running from the Plod, all he could do was, well, plod.

But this time he wasn't going half-cocked. He'd already snaffled two slices of bread and slapped sandwich paste into it. And now that Dad was back from the shops, he'd have his pick of crisps and biscuits. He had home clothes on – no uniform this time. He'd slept heavily last night so he felt a bit more alert.

Kevan wasn't sure how all this time-travel stuff worked but it seemed to function – partly, at least – on wishes. Or desperation. Perhaps his desire to be reunited with his bike would be enough. He'd spent all morning thinking about the tricks he did on it, pictured himself hugging it, even – in the hope that this would give him the power he needed. There was no thunderstorm today though, so if that was part of the cause, travelling wasn't guaranteed.

As far as he knew he could go back one day – 24 whole hours. He'd left his bike outside the library about 11am, which meant that he had to travel at 10:30 at the latest so that he would have enough time to get there on foot. Although he was travelling, this 24-hour thing was a bit of a challenge because whatever time he spent in Friday, would be the same amount of time he would be missing today. So he couldn't dither – he had to get his BMX, bring it back to the house, then travel back to today. If all went well, he should be back about 11:10. He didn't expect to need his packed lunch, but as his time in the Cubs and Scouts told him: "Be Prepared".

For that reason he had decided against taking £1.50 of pocket money and travelling back first thing in the morning to place it in the beans tin – that prolonged absence on a Saturday morning would certainly be noticed by his parents. And as he'd got up late, there was no point leaving it in the beans tin after 9am anyway – Kevan (#2?) wouldn't come back to check unless somehow signalled. He would just have to stay hungry. In the past. Besides which, he got a free breakfast anyway.

His rucksack was upstairs – the washing was about to stop so Mam would be in the back garden, and Dad would read the paper in his chair. Perfect.

He got his rucksack and went downstairs. He opened the inner door slowly, then closed it quietly behind him. He lay a hand on the door.

Hold on – if he went back to 10:30 Friday, and Mam and Dad were out, wouldn't the front door be locked? Mam said that she had a cuppa with Jackie, which wasn't true, but even if that woman in town hadn't been Mam, it didn't mean she hadn't gone out at all.

He opened the inner door and looked at the hook – no key.

Dad's would be in his pocket, but Mam's might be in her handbag. It was down by her chair.

The settee was squashed in by the door to the hall; then a lampstand and then Mam's armchair near the window. Dad's was in the corner by the arch, but as was the case with most Saturdays, Dad was led on the sofa, reading the back of the paper. Kevan walked in and sat down.

'Alright pal?'

'Yeah,' he said, a little too wearily, covering up his thudding heart.

'You don't sound like it.'

'Nah, I'm alright.' That was almost comatose – he wasn't blagging this very well. Winker Watson would not be impressed.

Kevan leaned to the side and felt the top of Mam's bag. He started unzipping it but the bag kept moving. He leant further over to hold the bag in place.

Dad lowered his paper.

'What are you doing?'

Kevan grunted.

'I think I've pulled a muscle.'

'Oh.' He raised his paper again.

The zip worked but it was loud. Kevan groaned louder to cover the sound. Dad lowered his paper again.

'You sure you're alright?'

'Yeah, no, I'm fine.'

The paper rose. Kevan rustled quietly until he felt cold metal. He raised the keys up and two of them jingled loudly. He groaned again, but it came out weird, like he was dying.

The paper dropped.

'What's going on, boy?'

'Ahh! Cramp!'

Dad put the paper on the settee and plonked his feet on the carpet.

'Do you want me to –'

'No, no, it's fine now.'

Kevan stood and walked to the door. Dad hesitantly reached for his newspaper, shaking his head.

'I'm going to play Metroid.'

'Ah. Okay.'

'Until lunch at the earliest.'

'Okay,' Dad said, peering at him. 'Still fighting that dinosaur alien thingy?'

'Yeah.'

'Alright, pal. Good luck.'

Already late, Kevan got to the porch, lay his hand on the door and closed his eyes.

That familiar rattle of rain heralded a successful trip. He peered through the inner door. He tried the outer door – it was locked. Mam was out.

Maybe she *was* that mysterious woman.

No time to wonder – she might come back any moment.

The rain on the porch was a welcome sound for all of one minute, until he unlocked the outer door and stepped out in it. He instantly felt the cold and it made him miserable, made him feel like he felt yesterday.

Just past the adventure playground, Kevan took Dad's clipboard out of his bag and threw it into a bush. Any attempt to sneak it back into Dad's possessions would create more problems than solutions. Besides, it was flaked with mud and a bit warped.

He had to get his BMX. It was battered, spotted with rust, discoloured and old – it was perfect. It did tricks and stunts like it was just part of Kevan's body. He felt it intuitively. It was like a pair of trainers he'd once got. He'd begged for some Reeboks but instead got some ProStar 1000s from the Sunday market. They looked horrid – but they were the best trainers he'd ever worn. He just pulled his joggers or jeans over the tongue and no-one could tell. And they were at their most comfortable just before they fell apart.

He had to get his bike back – and he almost hoped he would catch the thief in the act.

Kevan hotfooted it up the hill to the high street – his head and eyes flicking around for signs that he was 'crossing the path' of his other selves – but stopped briefly at the Bumptown Munchtown.

Mam was in there. Or at least, the woman Kevan suspected of being Mam

She had her back to the window, but while her coat was the same, they were a popular look and they sold cheaply on the market. And she looked a lot more hunched than Mam.

Kevan moved on. He was nearly out of time.

The casual clothes didn't seem to make a difference – he was still being stared at. And he was soaked to the bone all over again. It felt like it had rained three days non-stop, which for him was roughly true.

He got near the library at 11:24, sat in the bus shelter across the road, and waited.

'Ooh, this rain,' came an elderly voice beside him in the bus shelter.

'Yeah,' Kevan said absently.

The BMX was there, the handlebars still slightly luminous even in the rain.

'When is it going to stop?'

'Tonight. About quarter past eight.'

'Oh, okay. Thank you, young man.'

He perched forwards and scanned the streets for PC Richards.

'And what bus are you–'

'Sh-sh,' he said, harshly.

'Okay young man.'

He crossed the road and snuck up to the library wall. He grabbed the BMX, but before getting on it he decided to have a little peek in through the library window. There was Kevan... #2? busy at it. Well, busy reading about the colliery rather than writing about coal.

Then he saw the shell suit man on the other side of the library, reaching for the fire alarm–

And then it went off.

Shellsuit bustled out first, and froze when he saw Kevan. He glanced into the same window Kevan had. He seemed to be thinking of his next move – and decided.

He marched toward him.

And Kevan knew that whenever a grown-up did this, it was your cue to get out of there. He leapt on his BMX and pedalled. The man lunged for the bike, but Kevan just skimmed him and he fell onto his face.

Kevan turned down a side street and raced onto a road.

Why would that man set off the fire alarm? It just proved that grown-ups can misbehave just as much as–

Fast steps clattered out of the side-street. Was that him? And then an echoey *swish-swish-swish* from the shell suit as the man burst out onto the road and sprinted after him. Chase number three – Kevan almost rolled his eyes.

His heart pounded as he pedalled, his BMX waggling from side to side. He just needed E.T. in a basket and this would be over.

This didn't make any sense. Why was he being chased when it was Shellsuit who'd done wrong?

A powder blue Vauxhall Cavalier came out of a side road and screeched to a halt just as Kevan sped past. That was close.

Kevan turned down another alley.

He looked behind him as he neared the exit; Shellsuit entered the other end, running fast.

He got to the northwestern slopes and pedalled downhill, the wind at his back. Ahead, in the distance, stood the farmhouse, and the web of fields all around it, the western valley ridge a hazy undulating rampart.

The Cavalier was on the road behind him; was it just going the same way or was it following him to tell him off? Everyone was out to get him today – the police for truancy even though he was in school; supermarket security for being in their shop; Shellsuit for being caught doing something naughty; and now Cavalier man was after him for having the nerve to be nearly run over.

A flash of teal and magenta to his left; Shellsuit was sprinting through a lane of cottages. Kevan looked ahead – the road was winding round to skirt along the farmland and the weaker blossom petals from the cottage lane succumbed to the powerful gusts and swirled around him.

He passed the cottages – fields either side now. Drystone, hedgerow, layby, gates – all were a blur. But that was more to do with the weather than his speed. Kevan cycled as fast as he could in the rain, but the wind was now against him. Whenever he opened his mouth his breath was snatched. There was another flash of lightning; far above him the dark clouds seemed to be twisting, rotating with a thin dark finger extending down from them. Was that – was that a tornado forming?

There was a horrible crunching sound. Kevan looked behind. The Cavalier hadn't turned quickly enough and had scraped along the wall. A few stones at the top had fallen off but the Cavalier had clearly come off worse; its headlight had gone and the front bumper was flapping out at the side. Shellsuit was nowhere to be seen. Kevan started off again, looking ahead as hail started to sting his face.

More screeching and wrenching of metal – the Cavalier was forcing itself round, back onto the road, the wing badly mangled and the engine revving horribly, even though it was barely moving. More stones fell away onto the verge as the car eventually freed itself and came to rest in the road, the engine knocking. Shellsuit finally came out of the cluster of cottages on an old slip road, distinctive even from this distance because of his garish colours.

And then he got in the passenger side of the Cavalier, before it started to move.

Kevan's heart thumped hard. This had nothing to do with near-misses and fire alarms. It wouldn't surprise him if PC Richards and the security guards were in the back. He pedalled as fast as his legs could move, but they felt stiff and jerky.

Ahead the road gave way to the main Westgate Road. Left took him back up the hill and eventually to the high street gate, the supermarket, the bridge. Right took him further down, alongside the estate on the far side and farmland on the near, ending up in a nature reserve and then the creek.

More or less directly across was the entrance to Ya-Ya's housing estate, all tidy red semi- and detached houses with driveways and neat front gardens. Remaining woodland bunched around the collections of houses. If he could get across quickly, he could get into the trees and lose them, and then he could recover.

But simply dashing across the road would be dangerous. The road he was on was still narrow, the hedgerows giving no sight of the traffic on Westgate Road. Turning left would be safer – he could just skirt the gutter and hopefully he wouldn't get run over – but while turning right would mean having to dart across two lanes of traffic, he would get downhill speed and a chance to get lost in the nature reserve. He glanced back – they were gaining.

Lightning flashed. There was someone else, twenty metres ahead, cycling fast across the road with their arms protecting their head, into the estate entrance, where they promptly swerved and crashed into a bush in someone's front garden. The handlebars of their bike were a dirty yellow. Was that him? How was that possible? The figure looked back across the road – it *was* him, barely recognisable through a face contorted in sheer terror, but still him. Was it future him, or–

Then he too was crossing the road, and a large horn sounded and brakes squealed, and then the high headlights of a lorry blinded him as it thundered downhill toward him, and he raised his arms around his head as the engine grille was about smash into him–

Another lightning flash and the lorry was gone – or rather, it was halfway back up the road, speeding back down again. Kevan bounced onto the pavement, skidded across the same front garden and crashed into the bush. He looked around the lawn – future him was gone – and then looked back, just in time to see the lorry braking hard as past Kevan Bevan came across the road into its path and raised his arms. Kevan instinctively shut his eyes to the collision which never came.

A screech.

Hydraulics hissing.

A judder.

Past Kevan Bevan was gone. The lorry was jack-knifed further down the road, the smell of rubber acrid even from this distance.

The Vauxhall Cavalier was across the road, at the junction, smoke billowing out of the bonnet. Could they see him?

It indicated left, turned right, and pulled up to the back of the lorry. Kevan scrambled behind the bush just before both driver and Shellsuit got out. He peered through the leaves.

The driver seemed very angry – Shellsuit gave a slow, tired shrug. The driver raised his voice and shook his head. They both looked out to the housing estate; they didn't see him, but still approached the entrance, hands on hips, discussing their next move.

Kevan kept the bush between them, and quietly wheeled his bike into the woods.

★

Kevan got home and wheeled the BMX into the drive. He was about to fling it into the garden, but looked at the steel handlebar he was holding, wondering if it was a lightning conductor. If there was a chance that lightning caused time travel, that might explain his five-second lorry dodge.

Kevan wheeled it down the driveway to the garage, took off the padlock (which had rusted open years ago), propped the bike against a shelf and closed the door. He grimaced when he realised that he could have just done his homework *in here.*

Kevan entered the porch. 12:15. As long as Mam hadn't started lunch, they might not have noticed his absence. He'd missed the *ITV Chart Show*, but at least he had his BMX.

He peeked down the hall – he could hear Mam out back, humming a tune. Everything exactly as it was when he left. He climbed the stairs. He forgot he'd packed a picnic. Should he eat it now, or–

He could hear *Metroid* playing on his TV.

His heart started skipping – please don't say it's another Kevan. Is it past Kevan, he thought as he peered through the bannisters, or future Kevan?

It was Dad.

Kevan entered his bedroom. Dad was getting beaten up by some hopping alien.

'Thought I'd come up and have a go.'

He glanced at Kevan and resumed playing.

'It's a real achievement to get covered in mud when you're grounded.'

Kevan stood, frozen to the spot. He struggled to say anything. And then he remembered.

'I was just putting my BMX in the garage and I slipped on the grass and–'

Dad turned to Kevan, his eyebrows flat.

'You can try that crap with your Mam, but if you take advantage of our trust again, I'll give you a good hiding.'

Dad turned and carried on playing.

Kevan slowly shuffled to the bed and sat next to him.

Dad had never done that, would never do that. He only said it when Kevan had gone too far.

'How do I get through that little gap?'

Dad handed Kevan the controller. Kevan pressed down on the direction pad and the character turned into a ball, before rolling through the gap.

'Ah – that's how you do it.'

Kevan handed the controller back. Dad took it, and nudged him. Kevan smiled, fighting back tears.

# Chapter 19

Kevan sat in the back of the Sierra, the telegraph wires skimming across the sky, the drystone walls and hedgerows bumping up and down, coming near and dropping away with each junction, showing and hiding corrugated and slate rooves, silos and machinery, sheep and cows. Beyond, the rounded hills, variously covered with forest or fern, or grassed, with trees and hedge sprinkled at the crest. He couldn't remember if Gran's starchy, patched eiderdown reminded him of those hills or it was the other way round.

Fernvale was in a valley, but not that you could tell. They rarely skirted a ridgeline. There was no descending vista, no high, unruly horizon. And the sky was different here too – in Valley Hill the clouds seemed to rise up from the slopes and ridges around; here they hovered high and flat-bottomed, in little clusters. He would never say it but it made his heart sing.

Which was what he needed right now. He'd had yet another bad night's sleep. That made four in a row (well, three in a row by the calendar). The initial cause this time was Shellsuit. And although what he was wearing was nightmarish, it was more the way he chased Kevan.

He couldn't get the image out of his mind. The man burst out of the alley really fast and it made Kevan's heart skip every time he thought of it. And the briefest glance of the man's face was quite unnerving. He didn't look angry –

he just looked really determined. Almost robotic. Kevan closed his eyes tight and shook his head.

Who were those people? Were they still after him? Maybe they were detectives, out to get him. No, that made no sense. PC Richards was still chasing Kevan #2 when Shellsuit and Cavalier were pursuing him. As Mr Protheroe said, he hadn't even written it in his pocketbook, let alone alerted detectives to his truancy.

Maybe they saw him at the derelict terraces. He'd heard there were security guards patrolling near the mine, but he assumed they would be in black, or high-vis. Not shellsuits.

And although he was fine, he felt like he'd been hit by that lorry. Like it had happened and was then rewound. He struggled to comprehend what was happening. On the one hand, he'd gone back in time just before being hit by the lorry, which showed that if it wasn't the lightning, it was his survival instinct had caused him to travel. But on the other...

Seeing his future self, metres ahead, speeding across the road, had distracted him; if he hadn't seen that, he would probably have noticed the lorry and swerved up the road, avoiding it entirely.

And then it hit him – it was a loop. And these loops had been happening throughout.

He got splashed by a car, then went back in time, saw the car, and insulted the driver, who in turn saw him near a puddle and splashed him.

He had been able to get into school during break due to a pile-on which took Mrs Wells off the front step. A pile-on which his future self had gone back and created – but only because he'd seen that it got Mrs Wells away from the main entrance in the first place.

He had been able to escape the classroom because his future self had come in and distracted Mr Carter; but only because he'd seen his future self do that.

And worst of all, perhaps – he'd stolen his own BMX off himself.

They came off the 'A' road and wound around the side of a hill, passing slip roads and cottages, more farmhouses. Then the sign for the village. Past the village shop, the pub, the church set far back among a spacious graveyard and massive tree, and then a U-turn near the Midland Bank before parking along a small row of whitewashed cottages. Gran's was in the middle; the front yards were lined with a green cast iron railing but you could barely see it with Gran's – there were blooms galore bursting through already.

Mam opened the outer door, knocked and opened the inner one.

'In here,' came Gran's voice from the kitchen. Kevan stepped past the wellies and rough woven overcoat and inhaled the heady aroma of beef, dust and cigarette smoke all at once.

The feeling of going back in time touched Kevan when they passed the village sign, but felt especially acute whenever he came through Gran's inner door. The village shop had old, faded adverts from nearly ten years ago including the old "Nice Cold Ice Cold Milk" one. There was still the old red phone box – even in Bumptown they had the newer BT one. They went to the pub once and the jukebox had nothing from the mid-80s onward.

But Gran's house took him even further back.

The front room was actually everything bar the kitchen – a wide space with a dresser, bureau, dining table, hearth, old TV and a long-cushioned bench, a large wooden chair, and a winged armchair. There was no door to the kitchen but a step up; in the break between the two rooms was the chimney and opposite that the stairs. Ahead was the agar, with Gran bustling between that and the worktable.

'Gaw it's damp in here Mammy. It's not winter anymore – shouldn't I open a window?'

'Give over,' Gran said, and Mam replied in Welsh, and that's how they spoke until Mam kissed Gran on her cheek and came out of the kitchen, unbuttoning her coat.

'Where is he?' her voice sounded thick, like the way toffee curls back when bitten.

Kevan stepped into the kitchen and Gran enveloped him in her big arms. He rested the side of his head against her bosom and breathed in the TCP and starch through her blue Gingham overalls.

'Hello, Ratbag,' she murmured. 'You gonna help me mix the puds?'

On the heavy wooden worktable stood the Yorkshire Pudding mix, in a container with a handle on the side. She always left the pudding mix for him. At that stage the mix was flour, then a layer of eggs peeking out through milk. Kevan held his hand on the top and turned the handle as fast as he could. The whisks inside began to froth the batter.

'Not too fast darling – I don't want bubbles.'

Kevan finished and Gran ruffled his hair, and as they stepped down into the main room, she pulled out a Kinder Egg.

'That's for my lovely boy.'

Mam tutted as Kevan took it.

'Whoops – what's he done?'

Mam answered in Welsh. Gran responded in kind, and they were off again. Dad shrugged and switched on the telly. There were people protesting, people in uniform with riot shields.

'Is this those people from yesterday?' Kevan asked.

'No, pal,' Dad said, 'That was about the poll tax. These are prisoners.'

Some were sat on the rooves of the prison, standing, dancing, throwing roof tiles. Yesterday they were pushing against police in Trafalgar Square. Watching this in such a sleepy village, it felt like a million miles away.

Gran popped into the kitchen and came out with a can of Brains ale. She stopped by the wall clock, her brow furrowed. Mam noticed.

'You're going forward, Mammy.'

'Eh?'

'In time.'

Gran looked at her.

'I always forget.' And to Kevan: 'Hard to remember whether I'm going forward or backwards.' And she winked.

'Mammy, you're not ancient.'

'I do feel like it.'

'You're 59.'

'Swap those numbers and that's how old I feel.'

Dad was clamouring for the can of ale at this point so Gran handed it to him. He thanked her, pulled the ring off and tossed it into the wicker bin by the chair.

'Right Ratbag – get some newspapers from the scuttle.'

Kevan groaned. He knew what was coming. He went over to the hearth and picked up a pile of newspapers from under the matches. He took them over to the old dining table and laid the papers over the cover, the wad reminding him of the terrace he'd been in yesterday.

Gran got the Brasso tin, with its blue and white stripes and red top, and Kevan and Mam collected up all the brass – candlesticks, candleholders, carriage lights, jugs, tins, a large blanket box, ceramics with brass details, until the table was covered with many objects, all projecting a soft, yellow sheen.

Gran poured Brasso into three saucers and handed Kevan an old rag.

'Get cracking, Ratbag.'

Kevan began dipping the rag and wiping it over a candlestick; the shine turned to yellowy-grey smears, and the air took on a sharp, pungent tone. Mam and Gran did a lantern each and carried on talking in code. Kevan understood the odd Welsh word here or there, and they would sometimes use an English word or term, so he could follow the conversation in leaps. They were talking about the homework thing.

Then Mam's voice lowered and Gran stopped wiping. She responded short and Mam rolled her eyes and sighed.

'He said that, too,' she said, nodding over at Dad, who was twitching with excitement at the boxing.

Gran tapped Kevan with her moccasin slippers.

'Why do you think homework is a choice, Ratbag?'

Kevan carried on rubbing the candlestick.

'Your computer game will still be there when you've finished, boy.'

And to Mam:

'Those games are going to get more and more addictive, mark my words.' Another prediction from Gran. Someone had to mark her words about something most days.

Once the first phase was complete, Gran and Kevan walked to the village shop while the Brasso dried. ('That's the trick, boy. Let it dry and then the polish will be perfect.')

They entered the shop and Kevan picked up a six-month old computer magazine and gazed at Gran. She nodded – that was his reward for the relentless toil. Past the magazine in his hands, a selection of local and free newspapers sat on the lowest shelf. Kevan thought again of the papers under the brass. He thought about the abandoned terraces.

'What's on your mind, Ratbag?'

He hesitated. She picked up some OXO cubes and a lighter.

'Gran, what happened to Granddad?'

She looked at him with a little squint.

'No, I know he – he died. But… what happened?'

Gran walked over to the counter – a tiny square between the till and scales – and placed the shopping down. The shopkeeper served her and she bagged up and beckoned Kevan. Once outside, she motioned to the bench against the shop wall. He sat down and she sat next to him. She lit a long cigarette. She blew out a mass of smoke and smiled gently at him. She looked at her cigarette.

'They'd dug a new shaft but they rushed the men in to start work on it. The first shift was Good Friday, of all days. There were lots of problems with it, but the bosses insisted it was fine. When they were down on the first dig there was an explosion. Lots of men died. Some escaped. Others were trapped down there. Some of them were rescued but most of them were only found a week later when it was safe for them to be brought back up.'

'And… and those were all dead?'

Gran nodded.

'And Granddad was one of them.'

'One of ninety-two. Sorry – ninety-three: young Geraint died about five years ago. It would have been more but your Granddad saved lots of them with his quick thinking.'

She looked at him.

'But you know most of this, don't you boy?'

He nodded. 'But Mam never talks about it.'

'Ah. Well, it was her dad, you know.'

140

'Yeah – I know.'

'No, I just mean... it's much harder for her.'

'Oh.'

'You know, we felt the explosion on the other side of town? Up near the castle. They'd closed the school early so the children could go to the Green.

'I told Ruth to stay with Jackie and her mam, and Jackie's dad drove me back to the terraces to see what was going on. And it was chaos. Cars and vans everywhere, people running in different directions, mothers and wives wringing hands, men clumping around, helpless.

'And you know, the mine owners didn't even show up to the inquiry. They just sent some pale pair of glasses in a suit who weaselled out of every question. Somehow the company got away with it. They got a slap on the wrists and reopened about two months later. We were kicked out of our house because it was "tied", and the company weren't prepared to house us, as the only tenant who worked for them was dead.

'Good Friday,' she muttered.

She scraped off the cigarette ember with her fingers and placed the half-cigarette in her pocket.

'Listen Ratbag, I'm sure you want to know about your Granddad. It's only natural. Your Mam will talk to you about it at some point. It's just... well, it will have been 25 years in less than a fortnight. And Easter is always hard for her. You just need to give her time.'

'You don't seem, you don't seem...'

She turned and smirked, almost daring him to say it.

'... like, when Mam thinks about it, she's really sad, and sometimes she just sits there, like she's not even breathing.'

'And I'm not like that.' Gran nodded. She brushed ash from her skirt and placed her fists on her knees.

'Well, you know, it was a long, long time ago. And I think it hit your Mam really hard because she was just a young girl, about your age, and her dad was her world. And for reasons I will never understand, she still lives in Bumptown, which I don't think helps much.'

'Is that why you moved?'

Gran snorted.

'One of many reasons. Come on.'

They went back and polished all the brasses. They gleamed, all the reflections, gold black and brown. Mam opened more windows while Gran finished the roast.

Dinner was excellent as always. Thick slabs of grey brown beef, edged with dark-brown and black crispy bits, covered in dark gravy with rich bits of fat, batter crisp and beef crust in it, huge Yorkshire Puddings, into which Kevan poked a hole and then poured more gravy. He had six of those and about eight roast potatoes. Even her veg was nice. He ate all the carrot and green beans. For afters there was fruit salad, and then a homemade fairy cake. It had grated coconut in it, which Kevan normally hated, but Gran's light, moist and buttery sponge more than made it okay.

Dad snored in front of *Lawrence of Arabia*, while Kevan and Mam cleared the table. Later, Mam and Gran had a brief conversation; Mam shrugged, and Gran went upstairs. She reappeared with a big box, placed it on the table and lit a cigarette.

She opened the lid and pulled out documents, photographs, trinkets. Mam took a deep breath and smiled at Kevan. They began to sift through it.

There was a photo of Granddad, his top off, an ice cream in his hand, smiling. On the back: "Kevan, Aberystwyth, 1955". A picture of a young woman in a swimming costume, perched on a concrete wall, smiling too: "Enid, Aberystwyth,

1955". That was Gran, a woman that Kevan had never known wearing anything other than her overalls. Apart from in the wedding photo of them on the mantelpiece above the hearth. In fact, that was the only photo of Granddad in the house. There was one of her and Mam, as a baby, on the front sill. And there was about twenty of him dotted around the place.

He looked at the rest of them. Granddad and Gran together, in a tiny backyard, just like the terraces, his arm around her waist: "Kevan and Enid, Valley Hill, June 1961". Granddad in a tin bath, his face blackened; Gran by a stove, asleep in a chair. Some of Mam, a young girl, shy, arms behind her back, head cocked. Beautiful even then.

Another batch of photos – two men, one leaning on the other's shoulder: "Kevan and Dai, Valley Hill 1962".

Dai appeared in photos of other men, miners perhaps, and also in photos with Gran. There were some photos of three children, though these were tiny and hard to make out. In flowery writing on the back; "The Trio, 1944." Kevan still recognised them all – Granddad with his squashy face and widow's peak, Gran with her crooked smile, one cheek raised by it, her hair glossy. And Dai, like his adult self in the photos, a big, angular face, large eyes, large, bent nose, wide mouth.

There was a death certificate, something called an inquiry outcome, notice of eviction, marriage certificate.

Kevan asked questions, and for a lot of the time Mam watched Gran as she kindly answered in detail. Gran would sometimes answer and look at Mam as if to invite her to add to it; Mam would answer in one or two words, or purse her lips. Occasionally she would confirm details with a nod. But Kevan soaked it up. He didn't care who was telling him. They didn't talk about the disaster, but Kevan didn't care –

143

he was learning about the village Gran was from, where she met Granddad during the war, about mam as a small child.

Later, Kevan slouched in the other chair while Mam and Gran continued to talk in Welsh at the table. Dad woke in time to change from the film to *Rugby Special.* He flicked to the news before they left; more footage of the riot at the prison. Kevan lay down on the backseat on the way home – like he used to, on the way home from visiting his cousins in Bristol – unsure what to regret the most: the last Yorkshire, the last roast po, the second fairy cake. No-one spoke until they turned into Meifod Crescent, and then it was only Dad murmuring that he would put the kettle on.

# Chapter 20

The Sierra rattled into the drive about 7pm. Mam said she was going to bed; she unlocked the door, took off her coat and went upstairs. Dad suggested a film – *Top Secret!* It was one of Kevan's faves but he'd seen it a billion times. Besides, he had work to do.

Kevan retrieved his pad and the textbook, sat at the kitchen table and wrote his name and the date – Sunday 2$^{nd}$ April 1990.

'You sure you're not up for watching this pal?' Dad said as he sat in his chair, just visible by the arch between the dining bit and the living room.

'I'm okay Dad.'

He started writing.

'*Valley Hill Colliery was built in 1904 but it wasn't the first mine here. Valley Hill was mainly farmland but there was an ancient open mine past the creek at the bottom of the western slope and some of the legends were about how good the coal was and the magic properties it had–*'

Kevan sat back. He'd learned so much – it felt like the knowledge of reading, re-reading, writing, re-writing, and researching at the library, and talking with Gran and Mam, had finally hammered it into him – but he felt uneasy writing something so... official. Mr Carter had asked him to write about the coal. As long as what he wrote included that, the rest he would write as he pleased.

He screwed up the paper, tossed it over his shoulder like they did on telly – then picked it up and binned it on Dad's instruction – sat back at the table and started again:

*My Granddad Kevan and my Gran Enid moved to Valley Hill in 1952. Him and his best friend Dai got a job at Valley Hill Colliery. They worked in hard conditions with long hours with low pay. When they all striked, Kevan didn't because he had a baby who had polio before. Some people potted his windows*

'What are you doing?'

He looked up. Mam was stood at his shoulder, in her dressing gown. He didn't know what to say; he thought about her face at tea after they'd grounded him. He didn't know how she was going to react to things anymore. But she put her hand on his shoulder, and his mouth opened, and out came everything he wanted to say, about his conversation with Gran, about the photos they looked at, and that he didn't want to bother her, but there was something that just kept making him think about Granddad.

'I know Dad's family in Bristol, but I don't know our Wales family. Apart from Gran. And I don't want to ask you because I know you'll be upset. But when Gran talked about it today–'

'Okay, okay. It's okay. But why are you writing it down?'

'I'm writing this for Mr Carter.'

'Oh. Why?'

He shrugged.

'Did no one write about the disaster for their homework on Friday?'

'Dunno. He said that because of my family, I should write about coal, instead of the mine. No one read anything out loud about it.'

Mam nodded, but frowned.

146

'Well, your Dad's right. We don't know anything about coal.'

She read what he'd written. As she read, Kevan said, 'I think Mr Carter didn't want to upset any of us, talking about what happened at the mine. He said, "I know about your family and its... *history.*"'

Mam smiled at his impression and then nodded, but not a straight "yes" – she did that head-bobbing-around thing that Mr Carter did way back when. Thursday.

'He might have meant when Dad and others broke the strike as well.'

She handed Kevan's work back down to him and smiled. She moved to the sink, got a glass of water, and was about to walk back to the stairs, but she stood there for ages. Then she came back to the table.

She pulled out a chair and sat next to him. She looked out across the table, roughly toward the bureau.

'You know, I'd only had polio for a few weeks. Not that I could remember, I was only little. And thankfully it never came back. But when Dad broke the strike we had so much trouble for it, for years, and I'll never forget that. Others haven't either, even now, years later. When I was about eight, Dad came back from the pub with a swollen eye. He'd said he didn't know who punched him, but that might have been to stop Dai from retaliating.'

Kevan wasn't writing. He was just listening.

'And I never understood why me having polio would mean Dad wouldn't strike. Mammy later said it was just fear. Fear of what might happen. And a steady pay packet gave stability where there wasn't any normally.

'I hated that mine, hated how it made Dad feel. Dai would come round and talk unions and pay and hours and safety and Dad listened but that was partly because Dai was the only one who told Dad about it without having that look in his eye. That look of "Why do you care?" Or "Not that it's any of your business."

'Even Jackie's dad called my dad a scab; but Mammy said that she had given Jackie's mam a couple of shillings when the strike had entered the second week and because they didn't know how long it would go on for, they agreed she would give her some money every week to help. Turned out, the strike only lasted almost as long as my polio did, but where I fully recovered from that, our family didn't recover from *them*.

'We were made to feel shame. People whispered about us. I was bullied in the playground. Even the teachers were slow to step in when things got bad. And then I later realised that I wasn't ashamed of my family – I was ashamed of every other bugger in Bumptown.'

She looked at Kevan. Dad came into the kitchen to get a beer, but he did it slowly, and wasn't in a rush to get back to the film.

'I was your age when they dug out the new mine. They'd found another thick seam a few years after the strike. The company boasted that they'd dug it faster than any other mine here or in the South. Dai wasn't sure why they were proud of this; they'd cut corners, rushed the struts, there was poor ventilation. They were also starting the first drop on Friday, which was supposed to be bad luck. I was listening more, then. I cared what Dai said because hardly anyone else talked to Dad. And whenever Dad came back from his shift, and was asked how it had it gone, he'd shrug, or say "It's over", or "Another day done", and smile but in that weary way.

'They were in the first shift for the new mine; Dai had already said his piece but others were a lot more vocal about it. Dad kissed Mammy and me as usual, before leaving.'

Mam breathed heavily and gazed at the table. Dad stepped forward but said nothing.

'I'd made Dad... I'd made Dad a basket in school and then they let us go early. It was Good Friday. I was with Mammy, Jackie and her parents, playing games on the Green.'

'The green?'

'It was where the Memorial is now. We all felt a thud and a rumble. It was like that time you made me take you to the cinema to watch that film, do you remember, in Welshpool? When that thing blew up in the film?'

'We had to leave,' Kevan said, sad but beginning to comprehend. Mam smiled apologetically.

'Mammy made me wait with Jackie and her mam while she rushed off with the others. But I came after her half a minute later. Jackie's mam didn't try too hard to stop me.'

Mam started to well up but her voice sounded almost stronger as she fought through the wavering.

'I ran. All the way down the high street. Right across the four-way. Others were making their way as well.'

'I got to the mine gates; there were vans and cars everywhere. I couldn't see Mammy anywhere but I knew she was around.'

Mam wiped her eyes again, but the tears were simply running out of her. Kevan reached halfway across the table.

'–Mam, we can... we don't have to–'

Mam sat upright and clasped her hands.

'No, Kevan. It's not fair to have you creeping around here like you're on eggshells. You need to know. And I need to say it.'

Mam carried on talking, some of the time looking him in the eye with pure love, other times gazing at the bureau like she was in a trance. She told him about the not knowing, the endless waiting, the different buildings in the town being used for dark purposes – the community hall for a makeshift mortuary, the scout hut for the information centre, the mass funerals, with wakes in houses, people milling around. How people did attend her house, for Dad and for Dai, when the last lot were eventually recovered from the mine, how some people seemed to grudgingly respect Dad for his apparent heroism, talking like they forgave him for breaking the strike, and how she had yelled at them, saying they didn't want their forgiveness, that they could all go to hell.

'Which wasn't very polite, seeing as your Granddad was Catholic.'

She talked about how the company evicted all the widows within a month because there was nothing to be gained from housing them. And how they had moved in with Jackie's family. And how, long after the funerals, long after she and Gran became settled in their own terrace, the town hall for the official inquest was used. She talked about how Mammy and the others came out numb, shellshocked all over again,

She stopped talking, like that was where it all ended. Like the next part was a different chapter in her life. Kevan wanted to know more but Mam didn't look like she had any breath left in her. Dad hadn't moved, his can still unopened.

Kevan lowered his head.

'I'm sorry, Mam.'

She leant over, tilted his head back up with her hand and smiled.

'You haven't done anything wrong, my love.'

'But I should have talked to you about the homework, I should have–'

Mam shook her head, looked at the table, looked him in the eye and shrugged.

'What do I know about coal?' She kissed him sweetly on his forehead.

Later Mam went back upstairs, and Dad sat to watch more *Top Secret!* Kevan carried on writing. Once he put his pen down, Kevan Bevan had written eleven sides of A4, ranging from the strikes to the explosion, to the evictions, the inquiry, the closure, the boarded-up terraces. It all seemed a bit unwieldy, and he was still not entirely sure why he'd done it – or if indeed he would give it to Mr Carter – but there was a feeling of satisfaction, of making things right. His fingers and wrist ached from holding the biro. That didn't happen very often. It felt good.

'Kev?'

Dad was stood by the arch.

'You know I would never... actually... give you a good hiding.'

'I know, Dad.'

'My Dad...' Dad shifted his weight onto his other foot. 'Well, I just wanted you to know.'

'Okay, Dad.'

He took a breath and nodded to the telly.

'Nick Rivers is about to break into Flurgendorf prison dressed as a pantomime cow, if you're interested.'

He sat with Dad to catch the end of *Top Secret!* Dad looked at Kevan, smiled, and slouched further down in his chair. Kevan had seen this film a billion times before; in fact, he usually only watched old films with Dad, but they were some of his favourite times. It seemed to Kevan that whenever he was grounded, Dad tried his best to make his captivity as painless as possible.

After the film Dad put the news on – he didn't seem to notice that it was past Kevan's bedtime – but there was footage of the riot again, so Kevan went to bed anyway.

# Chapter 21

Kevan wanted to get his work onto the desk before Mr Carter could sit down. The teacher always held the door open for them; Kevan usually trailed the class but this morning he was third in. He put his work down on Mr Carter's desk, sat at his own, and rested his chin on his forearms, staring straight ahead. He briefly caught Mr Carter's eye, as he picked up the papers – he was frowning, and continued frowning as he glanced at Kevan.

'You alright?' Anish had said during break, for the seventh time. They'd already made up five seconds after he and Anish begun their trek to school.

'Yeah, I'm alright,' Kevan said. 'You alright?'

'Yeah, I'm alright. You alright?'

They'd given each other the sideways butt-kick and grinned impishly. Kevan looked out across the playground. Some kids from Year Five were playing Bulldog – there was a chain of about nine children and only two left to catch.

'I'm sorry, Dezzy.'

'What for?' Anish tried to sound confused but it wasn't convincing.

'You know – I've been a dill.'

'Okay,' Anish said, genuinely uncertain now.

'We're best buds forever, and I forgot that.'

'Okay.'

The chain had one left to catch.

'Just remember – if Ya-Ya comes near you, let me know.'

'You don't have to protect me, Bev.'

'Someone's got to!' Kevan said, but Anish looked a bit peeved, so he left it.

Mr Carter smiled at Kevan as they sat back down in class; strangely, Kevan regretted giving his work to him.

Later that morning, there came a familiar noise just beyond Anish's far side, but Kevan ignored it.

'Oi,' hissed Ya-Ya again. He rudely motioned for Anish to sit back so he could get Kevan's attention.

'What?'

'Saw Wrestlemania last night.'

'Oh, sod off, Ya-Ya.' Kevan said it as if exasperated at Ya-Ya's past failure to do said sodding off.

Ya-Ya glowered at him, and then the dinner bell rang.

'Kevan, can I speak with you?' Mr Carter said.

'But it's dinner,' Kevan protested, weakly.

The rest of the class piled out, followed slowly by Anish.

Kevan smiled kindly at him. 'I won't be long,' he said. Anish did his usual backing away, eyes wide as Mr Carter slowly closed the door on him.

He must have read it at first break. And now, he was going to have a 'chat'. Either that or he'd heard him tell Ya-Ya to sod off.

Mr Carter perched on his desk, gripped the edges, folded his arms, stuck them in his pocket. He then picked up Kevan's papers.

'Kevan, did your parents see this?'

Kevan nodded, did the head-bobbing thing.

'Kevan, this writing... ah...'

Mr Carter looked to the ceiling for a moment, and then found the word, so he looked back to Kevan.

'It's devastating.'

'Oh.'

'No, that's a good thing. Well, not a good thing–'

He put the papers down.

'It's the best work you've ever done.'

'Okay.' Kevan blushed and shrugged. Why did it feel as excruciating as getting told off?

'Mr Protheroe may want this displayed in his Visitor's Centre.'

'Okay.'

'I'm going to ring your mam in a minute, to ask for their permission. But first, we need yours.'

'My what?'

'Your permission.'

'Oh. Why?'

'Well, because the story… involves your family too. And… well, you wrote it.'

'Okay. Well, you are permissioned,' he said, with an aristocratic flourish.

'Now then – I can't take back your Action Slip, but I can give you one of these.'

He held up a Merit.

'Well done, Master Bevan.'

Kevan had seen one before, when Anish got one. He felt a pang of pride, but this time it was of himself and not Anish.

That pride lasted until the end of dinner when he overheard Ya-Ya, chatting with Hughesy as they filed back in.

'She said he puked everywhere.'

Kevan froze.

'And his name was Gavin?'

'That's what she said. He had on our tie. She said he'd yelled his name at them.'

'And then… and then he puked on them?'

'Yeah! All over her new trainers!'

'But Gav was in class.'

'You flippin' moron. Who cares who it was? She got puke all over her new white trainers. Cow deserved it.'

The spite. If Kevan had a sister – or a brother, for that matter – he wouldn't hate them like that. But he held his tongue, because he was in the clear. And that was fortunate, because you don't woo the love of your life by puking on them.

★

When Kevan got home he showed his parents the Merit. Mam smiled brightly, but her eyes were shining, like she'd been crying, or was about to. Dad held it like it was Wonka's Golden Ticket and Mam explained how Mr Carter had called her after her lunch, and she thought something terrible had happened, and she was already getting her coat to come up the school, when he explained why he was ringing, and that he said it was some of the best homework he'd seen all year.

There was that feeling again. It really wasn't that different than being told off. Kevan squirmed and shifted his weight from foot to foot, blushing all the while.

Dad murmured something to Mam, went out to the Sierra, came back in, and placed a videotape on top of the recorder.

'You're still grounded, pal, but you've earned this.'

Scotch Tape E-180. That meant 180 minutes, or three hours, of blank video tape. And on the edge label, written in big capitals, was the recording in question:

WRESTLEMANIA 6

Kevan's heart raced.
'Really? Can I watch it?'

'Yep.'

He picked up the tape. It was really here – he'd made it. After all the insanity of the last few days, he was still going to be able to watch it. After tea he was going to put it on.

The cogs started whirring.

'Can Anish come over?'

Dad looked at Mam. She nodded.

'Okay,' Kevan said, putting the tape back. 'Hopefully we can watch it tomorrow.'

'Well… you can ring him now if you want.'

'Dad, there's no need – I'll see him at school.'

'Yeah, but if you call him now… Kev, you've been looking forward to this for ages.'

'Yeah,' Kevan snorted, 'but Anish won't be able to come over at such short notice, will he?' He shook his head – surely everyone knew this.

'So after all this, all the stress, the grounding, the tears, the homework–'

'–and the blood and puke.'

'The what?'

'Oh. Nothing. Carry on.'

'What I mean is: after all that, you're going to leave it until tomorrow?'

'Yeah. It's only one more day.'

Mam and Dad smiled proudly for some reason.

There was a knock at the door; Dad grinned at Mam and went to answer it. Had he already invited Anish round? He heard a *click-clack* and a loud voice as he peered into the hallway.

And there stood Jackie, with Dad hanging up her coat.

'Thanks And,' she said. She always called him "And", even though he hated it. But Dad didn't seem to mind this time.

'Not sure what you two are gonna talk about seeing as you only saw each other Friday!' Dad said, as he walked through to the kitchen, his hand patting Mam's shoulder as he passed.

'Yeah,' Jackie said, making a face at Mam, and then she saw Kevan, and her eyes lit up and she pouted strangely.

'Hello stranger – long time no speak.'

For a moment Kevan had a pang of fear, but something inside made him temper it. Perhaps it was the adventures of late.

She took a step forward and nudged him gently with her hip when Mam turned to the kitchen, her voice low but full of humour.

'Don't worry, love – your secret's safe with me.'

Kevan was one day from his prize. Jackie and her bangles weren't getting in the way. He looked at her, tried to smirk, but he felt his cheeks and lips twitch awkwardly.

'So's yours,' Kevan said, gesturing to Mam.

She glanced at him, and smiled, but only with her mouth.

# Chapter 22

Tuesday. 8:30. 11 hours until "The Event". Kevan thundered down the stairs; the tape sat on the Videostar, unmoved from last night. He hoovered his cereal and hustled out, yelling a hasty goodbye over his shoulder. His body was acting like if he moved fast, time would move fast too.

He got his BMX from the garage, ragged it, and screeched to a halt so hard outside Anish's front garden that he was certain he'd made the pampas grass sway. Anish came down the path to him; because his parents disapproved of wrestling, Kevan barked out short sentences, only half-explaining the situation:

'Ask your mam to come over tonight. Dad got me a tape. I'm sure it will give you a "Mania".' He winked.

It had taken him the whole journey to Anish's to come up with that code at the end, so he was a little disappointed that Anish had already turned on his heel and ducked inside. But when he came back out, no words were needed. His wide eyes and slow, deliberate nodding said it all:

*We're on.*

They hung back near the Methodist Church, loitering near burgeoning apple blossoms until dead on 8:55 so that they could avoid "small-talk" in the playground. The moment the bell rang, they burst through the gates and lined up.

From the buzz in the classroom it seemed that very few classmates had seen Wrestlemania yet. Little Owen had taped and watched it Monday night – he'd brought the tape in to lend to Hughesy, and you could see Owen was fit to burst, trying so very, very hard not to talk about the matches, hopping around, making statements to Kevan and Anish that almost begged you to inquire further.

'There were some great matches...'

'Some surprises too...'

'Oh.. it was – it was... yeah, it was really good.'

Ya-Ya had watched it apparently, and also taped it, but he hadn't brought it in for anyone. That sounded about right. Kevan could hear him teasing Hughesy about it in class, telling him lots of silly things that clearly didn't happen, like there was a match where the ring was set on fire, or Gorilla Monsoon came dressed as an actual gorilla, and even though Hughesy knew it wasn't true, the joking had an edge to it, like Ya-Ya was desperate to spoil it too, and that it was only a matter of time.

10:30. Break time. T-minus nine hours. He and Anish huddled near the saplings, trying not to get drawn into any more talk about Wrestlemania. It had been exciting; it had been radical. Bodacious, even. They didn't need to hear any more.

And then, sure enough, Ya-Ya passed Kevan a note just before the dinner bell. He'd probably heard that they were watching it tonight and no doubt wanted to spoil it for them. Kevan screwed the note up and put it in his desk, all very efficient. Ya-Ya glared and his face went red, but Kevan didn't care – he wasn't taking any chances.

13:00. Dinnertime. This and afternoon break were the main risk points. It was technically T-minus seven hours (whatever T-minus meant) but in fact it was more like T-minus three hours: to home, and safety.

160

And then, less than a minute after they finished dinner and escaped into the playground, Ya-Ya found them by the saplings.

'Well, if you're not interested in Wrestlemania, I'll just tell you what happened shall I?'

Kevan didn't even answer. He just moved across the playground, leaving Ya-Ya by the trees. Anish marched at Kevan's shoulder. He wasn't even glancing at Kevan for validation.

'Beefcake beat Mr Perfect!'

Kevan stopped. A few heads turned. The playground quietened slightly, just the infant chatter and occasional squeal. Kevan looked quizzically at Anish, whose eyes widened: was Ya-Ya joking, or was he really doing this?

Kevan faced him.

Ya-Ya took a step forward, away from the saplings.

'Earthquake beat Hercules!'

He was.

He was doing it.

Ya-Ya was ruining Wrestlemania.

After everything Kevan had been through: the hunger, the tears, the cold, the Action slip, the Merit, the puke, the running – so much running – the grounding. The sodding *tornado*. And now Ya-Ya bloody Roberts was going to make it worth nothing.

Another step forward.

'Demolition beat Andre the Giant and Haku!'

Even Hughesy peeled away, his fingers in his ears, shouting 'La-la-la-la,' at the top of his voice. Even he could tell this was for real. Ya-Ya was going to ruin it for everyone just to ruin it for Kevan.

Kevan turned and marched on, to the side of the school, near the steps to the "Girls" door. Ya-Ya might destroy

161

Wrestlemania but Kevan wouldn't. No-one knew what that Merit made him feel. All he could do was walk away. And he was going to do just that.

Except he was getting to a dead-end. Red bricks down the side of the "Girls" door headed him off, like a Tron Lightcycle.

And then he realised. He could do more than walk away.

He had the porch. And he'd begged into it. And he'd travelled. But he'd also travelled without the porch. And if it was desperation that powered the time travel, then this was it.

He glanced behind him – Ya-Ya was quite a few paces back, and he was the nearest.

Kevan ducked around the steps and placed his hand against the wall.

He didn't say it out loud; he just wished.

'The Million-Dollar Man beat Jake "The Snake".'

That horrible, jarring squawk.

Kevan was still there. He hadn't travelled. And Ya-Ya was stood behind him. He was cornered.

Kevan wanted to scream. He wanted to thump Ya-Ya. He wanted to cry. Anish stood near, Little Owen on the other side, Ya-Ya in front, Jamie Williams behind. Hughesy marching in a circle beyond. But neither Owen nor Jamie seemed to be enjoying this. And they began saying so.

'The Hart Foundation beat The Bolsheviks.'

'Ya-Ya–'

'Dusty Rhodes–'

'–that's enough–'

'–beat Randy Savage!'

'Ya-Ya, come on–'

Ya-Ya took a step nearer, his face twisted with glee and hate.

'And in the match you've been looking forward to *all year*–' he shouted the last two words – 'between "Hacksaw" Jim Duggan and Dino Bravo–'

And then something happened. It took a moment for Kevan to realise why Ya-Ya had stopped, because it initially seemed like it was just a gust of air that caused Ya-Ya's fringe to blow sideways, but then a glob of spit smacked against his cheek, the impact spatter backlit by the April sun.

Kevan stared at Ya-Ya for an instant, then slowly followed the direction of the spit, as did Ya-Ya. Anish was wiping his chin, his eyes wide.

Ya-Ya slowly drew his wrist against his cheek, looked at it, then back at Anish.

Anish sidled past the steps, hopping and tripping over his own feet, his palms waggling in front of his chest.

'Sorry, Ya-Ya – it's just, you–'

Ya-Ya pushed Anish, and he staggered back. The crowd followed. Kevan kept close to Ya-Ya's back. He was still reeling from what Anish had done. For all the time Kevan had known him, Anish could only muster a string of spittle out of his mouth. Kevan had – with not a little practice – been able project little bullets of considerable speed and distance. But this one from Anish had speed and power. Kevan had even heard it on impact, like a short, sharp slap from a tiny hand.

Ya-Ya pushed Anish again, back into the main playground. Soon a larger crowd gathered. Ya-Ya then put him in a headlock.

'You think you can just do something like that – to me? And get away with it? You – of all people?'

He swung Anish around and his little legs flicked out. Kevan screamed.

163

'Stop it Ya-Ya! Leave him alone!' Kevan turned around wildly, looking for someone to intervene. Mrs Wells had come off her step, but too slowly for his liking. He saw Mr Carter at the window before he bolted out of sight.

This was it. Sod Wrestlemania. He was going to thump Ya-Ya, and he didn't care.

But then Anish slipped out, stood up behind Ya-Ya and put his arm around his neck. He squeezed. His eyes were wide but in a different way. Kevan wanted to cheer him, but Anish raised his right arm, gripped the crook with his left hand, and put his right hand on the back of Ya-Ya's head. Ya-Ya's face went pink. His expression was almost 'I'll wait patiently until you stop and then I'll batter you.'

But then Ya-Ya stopped struggling, and his brow and cheeks seemed to swell over his eyes slightly.

Mrs Wells hustled over.

'Stop it Anish!'

No response. Anish's gaze was fixed with determination, like he was focused on nothing else.

Ya-Ya's knees began to buckle and the two of them lowered to the floor, Anish on his knees, Ya-Ya's legs splayed out in front of him, but Anish didn't let go. Mrs Wells ran back to the main entrance, just as Mr Carter came storming out.

Kevan joined in, almost like a surprised parent: 'Dezzy, that's enough!'

Hughesy yelled: 'Stop it, you psycho!'

Anish glared at Hughesy and shrieked:

'My name... is–' and then his eyes flicked to Kevan – 'The Anishthetist!'

Mr Carter pushed Kevan and Owen to the side and prized Anish's arms off Ya-Ya's neck and head. Ya-Ya pitched forward, onto all fours, groggy. Anish sat for a moment, slowly coming out of some kind of trance, before bursting into tears. Kevan scrambled down and hugged him, but Anish pushed him away. Kevan slowly approached again, opened his arms once more, and Anish pounced forward and clung to him.

# Chapter 23

Kevan, Mam and Dad walked under the gate and onto the high street, together, for the first time in ages. It was Easter Monday, and, even though the disaster 25 years ago occurred on Good Friday, both this and the earlier event fell on the same date: 16th April ('Easter, like the bunny, hops around a bit', the Minister at the Methodist Church had once explained, as he scrubbed graffiti from the church sign).

Mam walked all wooden; Kevan linked arms with her, and he felt the pressure in the crook of his arm. She wore a nice dress with one of those inexplicably tiny cardigans that you couldn't fasten. Kevan had an Aztec print short-sleeved shirt and had even put gel in his hair. He'd cleaned his teeth vigorously this morning but they still ached due to the Easter Eggs from yesterday.

Jackie, her dad and her husband Malcolm came out of Bumptown Munchtown as they passed; Jackie kissed Mam on both cheeks and they followed behind.

'Is he the one who used to call Granddad a scab?' Kevan said to Dad.

Dad nodded and whispered in reply: 'A long time ago.'

Kevan looked around at him, at his red-rimmed eyes and red nose, as he brought up the rear. He couldn't help scowling.

Two grown-ups and a boy emerged from the new Arcade up ahead; standing awkwardly, seeming to loiter.

They saw Kevan's group and the man smiled, and Kevan's heart skipped when he recognised his bezzy.

It was Anish's final day of two weeks' grounding. Even though for the first few days of his grounding Kevan saw Anish at school, and Scouts, it wasn't the same, like visiting someone in prison or hospital.

Those remaining school days had been odd. Anish had got an Action Slip, as had Ya-Ya. The day after the sleeper-hold incident, Mrs Peters announced the creation of a new school rule: that children were not, under any circumstances, to strangle one another. She also took the opportunity to remind the children of an old rule: No Spitting.

And then a strange thing happened. Well, lots of strange things, but they all had a similar theme to them.

Ya-Ya was teasing Rachel over her spots in first break, and Little Owen told him to leave her alone. When Ya-Ya indignantly refused, Owen called him... well, a word for the male anatomy.

And then in second break, Ya-Ya invited Hughesy to his house for a sleepover, which was odd enough, but weirder still, when Hughesy accepted, he seemed to do it out of politeness.

And weirdest of the lot: Ya-Ya started ignoring Anish. Like, properly ignoring him.

The only thing that bothered Kevan was why Anish had pushed him away, after being pulled off Ya-Ya that day. He didn't want to ask, but he just couldn't understand it. It hurt. He was there for him and he'd felt rejected. Anish carried on as if it had never happened. Perhaps he hadn't realised it was Kevan straight away. That was probably it. Still...

Then came the first week of the Easter holidays and that was pure torture. Kevan had cycled around Bumptown, weaving, one-hand on the handlebar, the other resting on his leg. On one occasion Kevan saw Ya-Ya in his dad's butchers' – Ya-Ya seemed to slink down behind the counter. He'd also seen Gwen, with her friends, near the cenotaph again; no-one seemed to recognise him from before. Perhaps because he wasn't covered in mud, sweat and rain. But Gwen glanced for one second longer than normal. Not exactly a 'Who was that kid?', but it would do for now.

Bev and Dez played around as they made their way up the high street. Kevan didn't hear Mr or Mrs Desai speak to Mam and Dad but they smiled politely a lot as they walked behind.

'You all set for tomorrow?' Kevan asked as they passed the curtain shop.

'Definitely.' Then in a low voice: 'What film should I say we're watching?'

'Erm, I dunno.'

'It'll have to be "U" or a "PG".'

'Erm... "Star Wars"?'

'Which one?'

'I dunno, Dezzy. You choose.'

'Well, "Empire Strikes Back" is the best one–'

'But we're not actually watching it, are we?'

They got ahead of the grown-ups but stopped at the steps. Mam had slowed. Dad talked quietly to her. She nearly stopped, but Jackie and Anish's mam linked arms with her and managed to get her to walk further, the men following, their arms respectfully behind their backs.

When she approached the steps, she reached for Kevan, her wrist flapping, and he led her up.

Mam seemed unimpressed with the sculpture, preferring instead to touch the tulips and daffs; but she stood and took in the monolith near the top, her eyes wide and weary.

There were a couple of dozen people milling around it. Many were old, and they stopped talking and looked over at her.

Dad looked around, and Kevan followed his gaze. Jackie's dad stepped forward, put one hand at the small of Mam's back, the other at her elbow, and led her again up the steps.

'Why is he leading her up?' Kevan said, an edge to his voice.

'Because he organises the get-togethers.'

'So?'

'And he's asked Mam to come every year.'

Mam slowly reached the top of the steps. A man in his late-fifties spoke as she came near to the monolith.

'Is it… Ruth?'

Mam nodded. He approached, and she took a step back.

'Ruthie.' The man put his hands on her shoulders. She smiled. He embraced her gently.

'Who are they?'

Dad looked at him, smiling sadly.

'The survivors.'

'But Jackie's dad wasn't even down the mine when–'

'He didn't have to be. But he's still surviving it. They all are. Every day.'

Others began to come closer to her. Smiles, tears, touching, hugging. Even laughing, at times. But the older ones, the ones in their forties, fifties and sixties, were introducing their children, and grandchildren, to Mam.

'What are they doing?'

'They want your mam to meet their families.'

'Why?'

Dad bent down and put his arm around his shoulder.

'Because if it wasn't for her dad,' he said, trailing an index finger at the group above them, 'Some of them wouldn't exist.'

Kevan looked around. Mr Protheroe was stood by the gates, his face puffy through tears. Kevan held up a hand. He waved back. Kevan beckoned him over; he shook his head and smiled, before disappearing down the steps.

Kevan turned to Dad.

'If Jackie's dad asked her to come every year, why did she say yes this time?'

Dad put his mouth to the top of Kevan's head. He felt the moustache, the warmth.

'Because of you, pal.'

Dad kissed his head and ruffled his hair.

And for a brief moment before she began to search the monolith for his name, with the attention of the town on her, Kevan Bevan's mam seemed as tall as the conifers behind her.

# Chapter 24

Kevan had already eaten most of the chipsticks in the bowl before Anish came round, so Mam had to fill them back up. Dad was upstairs getting back into his jeans; he'd come down earlier in his undies and workboots, with some of Mam's makeup on his face. Kevan was embarrassed and reduced to hysterical tears at the same time.

Scotch Tape E-180; on the edge label: "WRESTLEMANIA 6". It sat on top of the Ferguson Videostar, awaiting the knock on the door. Kevan wondered if Dad's workmate had cut out the adverts like he did last year.

As he'd feared from the start, Kevan had found out all the remaining Wrestlemania results in the intervening fortnight. It was bound to happen – Little Owen couldn't stay shtum, and to be fair Kevan couldn't expect people to not talk about it. But once Owen started spilling the beans, Kevan had ushered him away from Anish so that he didn't overhear.

So, Kevan knew every result – but he wouldn't tell Anish that. He would pretend that he didn't know, just to make it still worth the wait. Because after everything Anish had been through, after everything he'd done for Kevan, it was the least he could do in return.

And in any case, Hacksaw won.

\*

Anish's dad drove him to Kevan's in silence. It had been an awkward goodbye to Mum at the door. She'd been the one to do the grounding; Dad seemed almost proud that he'd assaulted someone. She had initially said 'No' to him going to Kevan's, but Dad had overruled her for what might have been the first time ever. 'It's only "Star Wars",' he'd said. '"A New Hope",' Anish had added, and Dad gestured to him as if that reinforced his point.

Anish had heard all the wrestling results from Little Owen, but he wouldn't tell Kevan that. He didn't want to ruin it for him. And he wasn't really that disappointed, because – and this was something else he would probably never tell Kevan – he didn't really like wrestling. Although knowing the moves put him in good stead to deal with Ya-Ya that day. Maybe Bev was right; maybe Ya-Ya didn't usually watch it.

Dad did a twenty-seven-point turn in the turning circle and pulled in. Anish unbuckled and opened the door.

'Ani,' Dad said.

'Yeah?'

'Let me know who wins out of Hogan and Warrior,' he said, and winked.

Anish walked up the garden path, spotted with blossom. He raised a knuckle at the porch door and stopped.

What he *was* going to discuss with Bev – at some point, not tonight – was the events of that Friday afternoon. That when Kevan had pulled out the completed homework from his rucksack, there was that very same rucksack – complete with the same cartoons and biro graffiti – in a puddle behind him. And more importantly, when Anish had got home and calmed down enough to go to Bev's to make friends, he'd seen, amid the lightning on Meifod Crescent, two Kevan Bevans.

Ieuan flicked idly through his sister's *NME* mag while *Action Jackson* played on the TV. Carl Weathers was about to blow up some guy with a grenade launcher. ('Barbecue, huh? How d'ya like your ribs?')

Gwen was out as usual. Dad was in the back room, as usual. Ya-Ya had the living room to himself, as usual. He turned up the volume just as the man in the film started screaming. Dad didn't even bother calling out.

Ieuan put the magazine in his rucksack, heard a rustle. He pulled out a crumpled piece of paper: the note he'd left in Kevan's desk.

He hadn't wanted to ruin Wrestlemania for them. That wasn't his plan. He only tried to because Kevan had screwed up his note.

He should have just said it to Kevan instead of writing a note. He wasn't quite sure why 'Want to come to my house to watch Wrestlemania?' was so hard to just say, but there you go.

He screwed up the note once more and threw it on the floor among the crisp packets and sweet wrappers. Never again would he try to make friends with Kevan sodding Bevan.

★

The woman from the Memorial Gardens heard whoops and cheers behind the flashing curtain of 20 Meifod Crescent. She walked back, onto Old West Road.

She stood at the kerb; headlights seemed to flash at her from up the hill and she shielded her eyes. As it came nearer, she noted that it was a shiny new Ford Escort. A little less 'fiddly' than the now written-off Cavalier, but a bit more conspicuous as the production model in question hadn't even been made yet. And even more so as it was currently kangaroo-hopping down the hill.

It stopped abruptly a few metres past her. She opened the passenger door and leant in. She glanced at Laurel at the wheel, Hardy in the back.

'I'll drive.'

Laurel got out wordlessly and the woman got in the driver's seat. She slid the seat forward.

'You know, this car has power steering, fuel injection, and no choke.'

'It still has gears. It still has a steering wheel. It's still a faff,' Laurel said.

'Most people can still turn it round corners without smashing into drystone walls,' she said, adjusting the mirror. 'You'll be going back to Driving School before our next outing.'

She looked at Hardy in the backseat, winced at the garish shell suit that he was still wearing. 'And you're going back to Wardrobe.'

'Yes ma'am,' he said, sheepishly, tenderly touching his busted nose.

'And don't call me "Ma'am",' she said, indicating right. 'I needn't remind you that this isn't the fifties.'

She handed the homework to Laurel.

'What am I doing with this?' he said.

'Get rid.'

'Are we back on track?' he said, as the homework shrivelled, darkened and turned to smoke in his hands.

'For now,' she murmured, checking her mirrors. 'But I've got a feeling we'll be coming back.'

The Escort did a neat U-turn and climbed the hill, bound for the bridge.